CHOOSE YOUR

STAR WARS™

AN OBI-WAN & ANAKIN ADVENTURE

WRITTEN BY

CAVAN SCOTT

ILLUSTRATED BY

ELSA CHARRETIER

LOS ANGELES • NEW YORK

For information address Disney • Lucasfilm Press,
1200 Grand Central Avenue, Glendale, California 91201.
Printed in the United States of America
First Paperback Edition, March 2019
1 3 5 7 9 10 8 6 4 2
FAC-029261-19043
ISBN 978-1-368-04337-3
Library of Congress Control Number on file
Designed by Leigh Zieske

Visit the official *Star Wars* website at: www.starwars.com.

» ATTENTION, READER

Obi-Wan Kenobi and Anakin Skywalker
are two of the galaxy's greatest Jedi–
but they need your help!

This book is full of choices—choices that lead
to different adventures, choices that you must
make to help Obi-Wan and Anakin.

Do not read the following pages straight through
from start to finish! When you are asked to make
a choice, follow the instructions to see where that
choice will lead Obi-Wan and Anakin next.

CHOOSE CAREFULLY.

AND MAY THE FORCE BE WITH YOU!

A LONG TIME AGO
IN A GALAXY FAR, FAR
AWAY. . . .

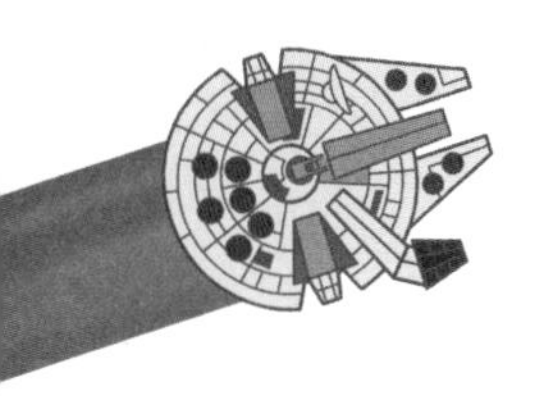

ANAKIN SKYWALKER'S lightsaber blazed to life. He leaned back in a defensive stance just as he'd been taught—blade forward, free hand raised palm out. He narrowed his eyes, ready for attack, a confident smile on his lips.

Bring. It. On.

The smile dropped away as his lightsaber was yanked from his fingers. The sizzling blade cut out as the weapon pinwheeled through the air to land in his opponent's hand.

"Master?"

Obi-Wan Kenobi clipped Anakin's lightsaber to his belt. The Jedi Knight didn't speak, his piercing blue eyes studying Anakin's expression.

"Master," Anakin repeated. "I thought we were training."

"We are, my young Padawan," Obi-Wan replied. There was a hum as three training remotes zipped into the Jedi Temple's training gallery. The spherical drones hovered around Obi-Wan, lights flashing across their polished surfaces. They looked innocent enough, but

Anakin had learned the hard way that every remote could deliver a painful laser sting.

"But how am I supposed to defend myself without a weapon?"

Obi-Wan flicked a wrist, and a wooden staff flew from a chest near the far wall. Anakin caught it, looking at his master in disbelief.

"A training sword? I haven't used one of these for years. . . ."

"Long before you constructed your lightsaber, yes."

"Then why—"

The Jedi Knight didn't let Anakin complete his question. "You rely too much on your lightsaber, Anakin. It makes you sloppy."

Anakin's cheeks burned at the accusation. "Sloppy? You always say my lightsaber is my *life*."

"You are becoming complacent. A lightsaber is an elegant weapon, but it is only a tool. And tools fail, usually when you need them most."

Anakin indicated the floating remotes. "But a wooden stick against training remotes? They'll burn it to pieces."

A voice rang out behind him. "Survive it will, in the right hands."

Anakin turned to see a group watching him from beneath one of the gallery's many arches.

“Master Yoda,” Obi-Wan said, spotting the wizened alien. “We weren’t expecting you.”

“Passing we were,” Yoda said. “Continue, you should, as if here we are not.”

That was easier said than done. Being watched by one legendary Jedi was bad enough, but Yoda wasn’t alone. A Mon Calamari stood beside the Jedi Master’s hoverchair: Bant Eerin, one of Obi-Wan’s oldest friends in the temple. And there was no mistaking the figure coming from the holoprojector held in Bant’s webbed fingers: Mace Windu’s steely gaze was unwavering even as a hologram.

Obi-Wan turned his attention back to his apprentice. “Anakin, are you ready?”

How can I be? Anakin thought. It was bad enough that Obi-Wan was making him fight with a trainee sword, but in front of a group of senior Jedi . . .

His eyes sparkled. Perhaps it was time to teach his *master* a lesson!

WHAT SHOULD ANAKIN DO?

USE THE FORCE TO STEAL OBI-WAN’S LIGHTSABER—**TURN TO PAGE 25.**

USE THE FORCE TO DESTROY THE REMOTES—**TURN TO PAGE 17.**

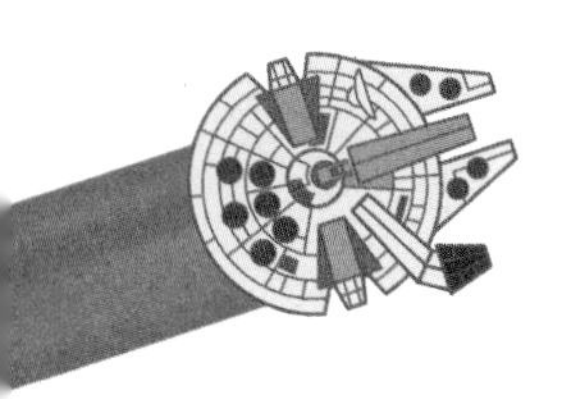

"I'M SORRY, MASTER," Anakin said, running for the exit, "but I have to do this."

Obi-Wan called after him, but the words were lost in the sounds of blaster fire and whirling energy blades.

Anakin jumped into a turbolift and was grateful when it sped upward. He didn't like the idea of having to climb all the way back to the top of the temple. Still, the ascent seemed to take far too long. Anakin paced the small chamber, urging the turbolift to go faster, his stomach knotted with dread. What if he was too late?

The door pinged open and he raced to the lift that would spirit him up to the Council Chamber. A Temple Guard was sprawled unconscious in front of the open doors.

Anakin hesitated. Should he make sure the guard was okay or continue to the Council Chamber? If the Council was really in danger . . .

SHOULD ANAKIN MAKE SURE THE GUARD IS OKAY?

YES—TURN TO PAGE 11.

NO—GO TO PAGE 40.

ANAKIN TRUDGED BACK into the training gallery. With a bellow of frustration, he lobbed a training remote at the wall . . . but Yoda caught it before it could smash into pieces.

"Careful you must be. Anger leads to hate. Hate—"

Anakin wasn't in the mood for a lecture. "Leads to the dark side. Yeah, I know."

"Yet still you do not learn."

"But it's not fair—"

"Not fair. Not fair." Yoda shook his head. "Always talking. Never listening."

"But what if it's not me who needs to listen?" Anakin said, looking away from Yoda.

"Patience, you must have," Yoda said. "Earn Kenobi's respect, you will."

"When?" Anakin scoffed, turning to face the Jedi Master, but Yoda was gone.

THE END

CAN YOU HELP ANAKIN MAKE BETTER CHOICES?

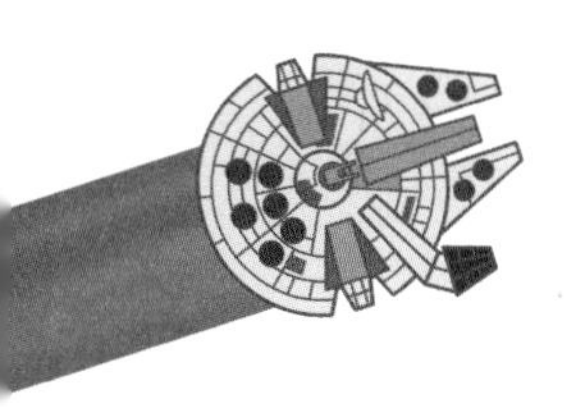

THE BLARE OF A SPEEDER HORN made him look down. An air taxi was zipping through Coruscant's busy skylanes, swerving in and out of traffic to pick up a new fare.

Anakin jumped from the window, landing in the back of the open cab.

"Sorry, pal," the driver droid said. "I'm booked. You're going to have to find yourself a new ride."

"No time for that," Anakin said, throwing the droid over the side.

Anakin leapt behind the controls and pulled up on the flight stick. The air taxi shot up, narrowly missing a speeding skyhopper.

Warning lights flashed on the dashboard, a computerized voice advising that he was pushing the repulsors way past acceptable safety limits. Anakin killed the warning, diverting all available power to the thrusters.

The turbines squealed in protest, but he gunned the engine for all it was worth. With a splutter, the antigrav unit gave out. Anakin held on as gravity took hold, the guard's freighter rocketing away.

The air taxi fell into the path of a bulky cargo transporter, and the wedge-shaped truck clipped the back of the taxi. It went into a spin, and Anakin wrestled to pull it out of its dive. It was useless. His only option was to jump.

He let go of the flight stick and was preparing to fling himself over the edge when the taxi jerked to a halt. It hung in the air, blue lights reflecting off its scuffed paintwork as a sleek gunship rose in front of it.

Anakin groaned as he recognized the Coruscant Security Force emblem and heard a police droid's voice booming over the loudspeakers.

"You are being held in a tractor beam. Drop all weapons and surrender."

"Master Yoda has been kidnapped from the Jedi Temple!" Anakin yelled up at the blue-plated droid. "He's in that ship up there."

He glanced up. The guard's ship was nowhere to be seen.

"We could still track them," Anakin said, but the police droid wasn't listening.

"You are under arrest."

"On what charge?"

"Stealing an air taxi and reckless flying."

"I don't have time for this!"

"Do you want to add resisting arrest to the charge sheet?"

Anakin slumped back in his seat and let the taxi be towed to the nearest station. What was the point? The guard's ship would be light-years away by now.

THE END

CAN YOU HELP ANAKIN MAKE BETTER CHOICES?

ANAKIN SWUNG ONTO the ladder and started clambering down.

Something cracked beneath his boot. His foot went through a rung, the metal corroded and brittle. He cried out as he lost his grip and tumbled down the shaft. He pushed out to either side, using the Force to slow his descent.

He jolted to a halt, hanging midair. He had no idea how far he'd fallen or whether there was another exit in reach.

Anakin threw back his head and yelled for help.

THE END

CAN YOU HELP ANAKIN MAKE BETTER CHOICES?

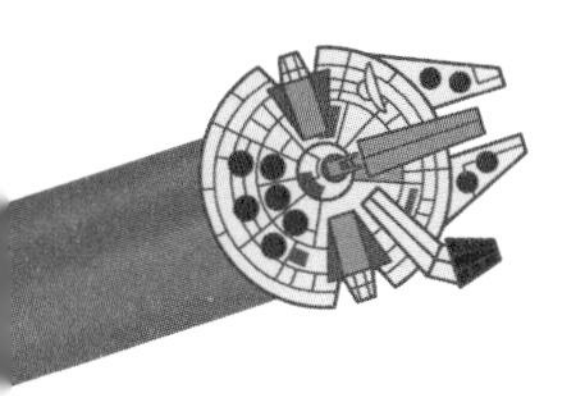

ANAKIN RAN to the slumped figure, feeling the guard's neck to check for a pulse. His fingers found only cold metal.

The guard's head snapped around, the mask falling away to reveal the beaked face of a battle droid. Green gas streamed from the robot's vocoder. Anakin coughed, taking in the acrid smoke. He tried to stand, but the corridor whirled around him. He tumbled to the ground, darkness rushing in.

THE END

CAN YOU HELP ANAKIN MAKE BETTER CHOICES?

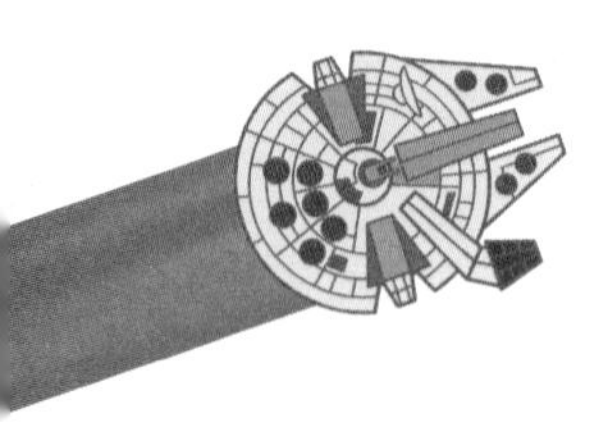

ANAKIN DID AS HE WAS TOLD and instantly regretted the decision. The guard raised his arm, revealing a dart gun fitted snugly to his wrist. A dart struck Yoda in the neck, and the Jedi Master slumped to the floor.

Before Anakin could react, the guard whirled around and Anakin felt the sting of a dart in his own arm. His knees buckled, and he collapsed where he stood.

TURN TO PAGE 36.

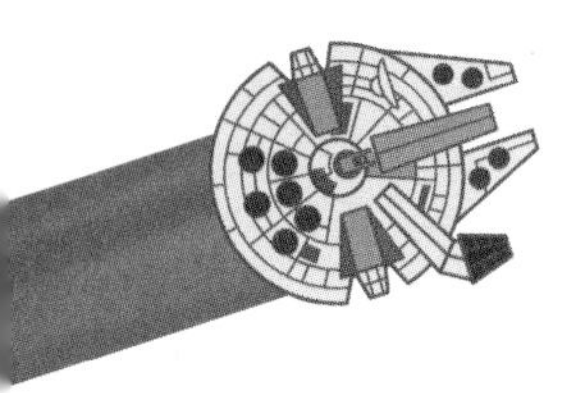

"TOO LONG," ANAKIN SIGHED, reaching across to test the ladder's strength.

Then an idea occurred to him, a plan so ridiculous that Obi-Wan would never allow it.

So he *had* to do it.

Anakin hurried back to the gallery and snatched a remote from the crate. Reaching for a pouch on his belt, Anakin pulled out the tiny bit driver he'd used ever since constructing C-3PO as a kid. Plunging the tool into the remote's control module, he started to reprogram the drone.

Minutes later, Anakin was back at the service duct with not one but two hacked remotes hovering beside him. Anakin pulled back the drape and nodded expectantly at the empty shaft.

"Well? What are you waiting for?"

The reprogrammed drones buzzed into the space, their lights illuminating the vertical tunnel. They dropped down until they were level with Anakin's feet and—before he could change his mind—he stepped forward, placing his left foot on the nearest remote. The drone dipped slightly but remained in the air. Using a ladder rung for support, Anakin cautiously stepped onto the other drone.

Letting go of the ladder, Anakin threw his arms wide to maintain his balance. He laughed out loud as the remotes took his weight, hovering in the air. Yes, there'd been a *small* chance he would plunge to his doom, but the thought of getting one over on Obi-Wan had made it worth the risk.

"All right, down we go."

The remotes dropped down the shaft, Anakin riding them like a skimboard. They performed perfectly, although their repulsors soon began to whine. The whine turned into a shriek as Anakin guided them farther into the shaft that led down to the storage level.

"You can do it," Anakin encouraged the remotes as the grate at the bottom of the shaft came into view. "You can do it!"

As if to prove him wrong, the drone beneath his right boot sparked and fizzed before cutting out completely. Anakin tumbled toward the grate, grunting as he smashed through the metal to fall into a room full of towering shelves. Flipping over, he pushed down with the Force to cushion his landing.

Anakin jerked to a halt, suspended centimeters from the cold, hard floor. He caught his breath, but the second remote failed high above him and tumbled

down the shaft to smack into the back of his head. The shock broke Anakin's concentration and he slapped to the ground. He laughed, rolling onto his back to see the shattered grate high above.

He'd made it . . . but where were the intruders?

And where were Obi-Wan and the guards?

He scrambled up, using the Force to grab the defunct remote from the ground. It wasn't much of a weapon, but it was the only one he had.

Anakin looked around. The air was fragrant, perfumed by crates full of fresh vegetables and dried herbs. He'd landed in a pantry. His eye fell on a tray of purple peaches, each the size of the training remote he held in his left hand.

"Don't mind if I do," he said, selecting the largest peach and biting into its flesh as he crept through the stacks, juice running down his chin. He'd have to remember that place if he was ever in need of a midnight snack.

He was almost finished with the peach when he found a door that led into a featureless corridor. Sucking pulp from his fingers, he tossed the pit aside and snuck out into the hallway. That far down there was no need for the ornate decorations of the main temple. No tapestries adorned those walls. There were just metal doors leading to other gloomy storerooms.

Where was the intruder? Where should he search?

Anakin closed his eyes. The Force would be his guide.

WHERE SHOULD ANAKIN INVESTIGATE FIRST?

THE LINEN STORES—GO TO PAGE 38.

THE TRAINING STORES—GO TO PAGE 30.

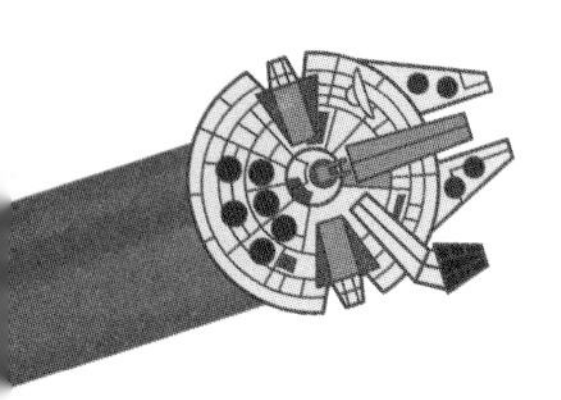

ANAKIN FLUNG OUT HIS ARMS and pushed with the Force in all directions. Obi-Wan was knocked off his feet as a wave of raw energy swept through the remotes, smashing them into the walls.

"Anakin, no!"

His master's warning came too late. Cracks spiderwebbed across the walls, and pillars shattered to dust. With a roar, the gallery's vaulted ceiling collapsed on itself.

Anakin ran, expecting to be crushed beneath falling masonry any moment, but no debris reached the floor. He looked up to see the rubble suspended in the air.

Master Yoda stood on his hoverchair, arms raised. He had saved them from being crushed, but disappointment was etched across his face.

With a flick of his wrists, the debris spun safely out of the way.

Obi-Wan stared at Anakin in disbelief. "What have you done?"

Shame burned in Anakin's chest. The training gallery lay in ruins, all because of him.

“I’m sorry, Master . . .” he mumbled, unable to meet Obi-Wan’s eyes.

“I should think so. How many times, Anakin . . . ? You must learn to control your emotions.”

“I’m trying, but . . .”

He paused at the sound of Master Yoda’s hoverchair floating toward them. He already knew what the Jedi Master was going to say.

“Do or do not . . .” Yoda began.

“There is no try,” Anakin muttered, completing Yoda’s oft-repeated mantra.

The Jedi Master huffed, glancing around the wreckage. Behind them, Bant was already calling for maintenance droids.

“Help the droids you will,” Yoda said.

Anakin’s shoulders slumped. “Do I have to?”

“Anakin,” Obi-Wan snapped. “This is your mess. You must clean it up.”

“But my training—”

“Will wait until the work is completed.”

“Maybe think twice next time, you will,” Yoda said as the Jedi Masters left Anakin with his thoughts . . . and his regrets.

THE END

CAN YOU HELP ANAKIN MAKE BETTER CHOICES?

"BUT YOU ALWAYS TELL ME to trust my instincts," Anakin said.

"Anakin!" Obi-Wan said, blocking another barrage of lasers. "This isn't the time to argue!"

"Very well," Anakin said, launching himself at the nearest droid.

The stacks echoed with the sound of whirling lightsabers. Soon Obi-Wan and Anakin were surrounded by scrapped droids.

Anakin looked at his master expectantly. "Now can we check on the Council Chamber?"

But when they got there they found the windows smashed and the chamber in disarray.

A lightsaber lay in the middle of a blaster-scorched floor.

Master Yoda's lightsaber.

Obi-Wan looked at the devastation in disbelief. "What happened here?"

"I told you I sensed danger!" Anakin said, turning on his master.

"We were in danger ourselves."

"From a few second-rate droids?" Anakin yelled,

lashing out with the Force. Obi-Wan flew back and slammed against the wall. He slid unconscious to the floor.

"What have you done?" came a voice behind him. Anakin whirled around to see a hologram of Mace Windu staring at him in dismay.

"There was a break-in. Obi-Wan—"

"I saw what happened to Obi-Wan," Mace said, cutting him off. "Return to your quarters."

"Master?"

"You will have no part in this investigation. Argue, and you will have no part in this Order!"

Disgraced, Anakin fled from the Council Chamber, the Jedi's words ringing in his ears.

THE END

CAN YOU HELP ANAKIN MAKE BETTER CHOICES?

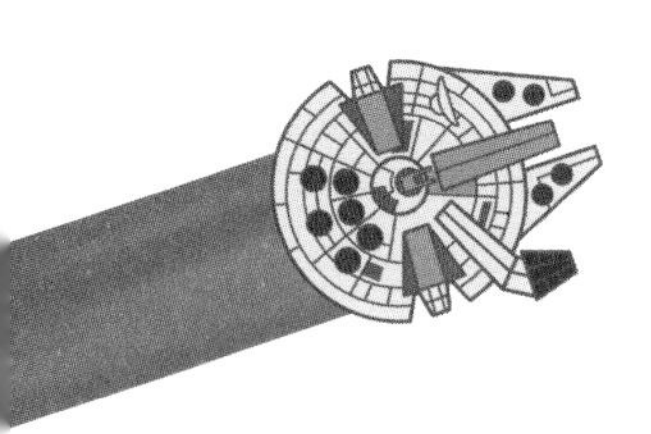

ANAKIN IGNORED THE COMMAND, drawing his lightsaber. The guard leapt back to his feet, blocking the Padawan's sizzling blade. Their lightsabers clashed again and again as they circled each other. Try as he might, Anakin couldn't get near the masked man.

Finally, Anakin got lucky, cleaving the guard's hilt in two. The victory was short-lived. The guard's gloved hand snapped up, and Anakin was thrown back against the wall. He was pinned in place, barely able to breathe, let alone move. He didn't even have his lightsaber. It lay at the guard's feet alongside the bisected pike. The lightsaber twitched on the ground as Anakin tried to summon it, the pressure on his chest too great.

A battered freighter rose into view outside the arched window, accompanied by four battle droids, each wearing a jet pack. The droids fired, shattering the windows. Glistening shards whistled across the chamber. Anakin turned his head, expecting to be cut to ribbons any second. Instead, the razor-sharp fragments tinkled to the wooden floor, deflected by an unseen barrier. Someone had protected him. Master Yoda?

He opened his eyes to see the Grand Master lying stunned on the floor, his lightsaber discarded.

"No," Anakin croaked as two droids plucked the unconscious Jedi from the ground. "Don't touch him."

They didn't listen, flying the Jedi Master over to the waiting freighter. Anakin cried out in frustration, his lightsaber finally snapping to his waiting hand. He was armed but still fixed to the wall, unable to break free.

"You should have listened to your master," the guard growled, scooping up the two halves of his lightsaber pike, his voice rendered unrecognizable by a modulator.

"Where are you taking him?" Anakin spat.

"Far away from here. Why? Are you going to stop me?"

"You can count on it."

The guard chuckled. "I like you, kid. And you're not bad with a saber. It's a shame we have to kill you."

Anakin tumbled forward, suddenly released from the Force grip as the guard ordered the droids to fire.

"Roger, roger," they acknowledged, metal fingers squeezing their triggers.

Anakin rolled into the blaster bolts, bringing up

his lightsaber to protect himself. The guard raced for the window and leapt onto the freighter. He turned to glance back as the repulsors thundered and the ship rocketed out of view.

There was no time to lose. Anakin swiped his hand across the advancing battle droids, sending them crashing into each other.

"Hey, watch it," they complained as Anakin swept his lightsaber in a wide arc, slicing them in two.

Anakin ran to the smashed window. The guard's ship was disappearing into the clouds, its thrusters glowing brightly against the darkening sky. He had to go after it, but how?

HOW SHOULD ANAKIN CHASE THE SHIP?

USE A JET PACK—TURN TO PAGE 70.

USE A SPEEDER—GO TO PAGE 7.

OBI-WAN GASPED in surprise as his lightsaber flew to Anakin's outstretched hand. The remotes darted forward as Anakin activated the blue blade, the nearest firing a bright yellow bolt at the Padawan's chest. Anakin brought Obi-Wan's saber up, deflecting the bolt into the second remote. It dropped to the floor, its systems shorting out.

One down, two to go.

Throwing his wooden sword aside, Anakin swung at the second remote. The blade sliced through the drone as if it was camba-fruit.

"Anakin!" Obi-Wan scolded as the smoking halves clattered to the ground. "You're only supposed to block, not attack!"

That'll teach you to embarrass me in front of the Masters, Anakin thought as he lunged forward, spearing the remaining remote through its core.

Anakin extinguished the blade, and the impaled drone dropped to the floor.

He smirked at Obi-Wan. "Are we done, Master?"

The Jedi's face was like stone. "Hardly," he replied, waving a couple of fingers in the air. Remotes flew

in from every angle to surround Anakin. He pivoted, reigniting his stolen blade as the drones opened fire. Lasers struck Anakin's arms and back. He swiped at the nearest remote, but it darted clear of his blade to deliver a stinging blast to his shoulder. Another beam hit him in the small of his back. He swung around but lost his footing as another remote stung his hand. Anakin yelped, dropping Obi-Wan's lightsaber. The hilt never reached the floor. Obi-Wan simply raised a hand, calling his weapon back to him.

"Enough!" Anakin gasped, the remotes swarming around him like redjacket wasps. "I'm done."

"That is an understatement," Obi-Wan said. The remotes paused, waiting obediently for their next command. "You stole my lightsaber."

Anakin rubbed his aching shoulder. "I took initiative. I thought you'd be pleased."

"Pleased? Anakin, you were *angry*."

"Can you blame me? You were treating me like a youngling."

"So you decided to act like one? The training gallery is no place for tantrums. You didn't want to pass the test. You wanted to embarrass me in front of Master Yoda."

"That's what you were doing to me! It's not fair!"

Out of the corner of his eye, Anakin saw Yoda shake his head. The Jedi Masters turned and left.

He sighed, closing his eyes. Obi-Wan was right. He *had* been angry. He'd been furious. But yelling didn't help. He uncurled his fists, opening his eyes to see the remotes packing themselves into the training crate.

"Master, I—"

Obi-Wan silenced him with a worried look. "Anakin, wait. Do you feel it?"

Anakin reached out with the Force. "Yes. Something's wrong," he said, their quarrel forgotten.

They ran through the exit to see Temple Guards racing down the corridor, lightsaber pikes in hand.

"What's happening?" Obi-Wan asked.

"There's been a break-in," the nearest guard replied.

"In the temple? That's impossible."

"Tell that to whoever's sneaking around the storage level."

The guard continued after his colleagues. Anakin suppressed a shiver. Temple Guards always put him on edge. It was something about the featureless masks they all wore. Anakin had a hard time trusting anyone who hid their face. It reminded him too much of the Sand People back home.

The guards reached a turbolift at the end of the corridor. Obi-Wan called for them to wait, chasing after them, Anakin at his heels.

"No, Anakin," he said, pausing by the turbolift door. "You wait here."

"But I want to help!"

"And I want you to stay back this time. Clean up the practice gallery. Make sure everything is back where it belongs by the time I return—including the remotes you destroyed."

"But, Master—"

Obi-Wan stepped into the turbolift, and the doors closed before Anakin could finish his sentence.

SHOULD ANAKIN DO WHAT OBI-WAN SAYS?

YES—TURN TO PAGE 6.

NO—TURN TO PAGE 42.

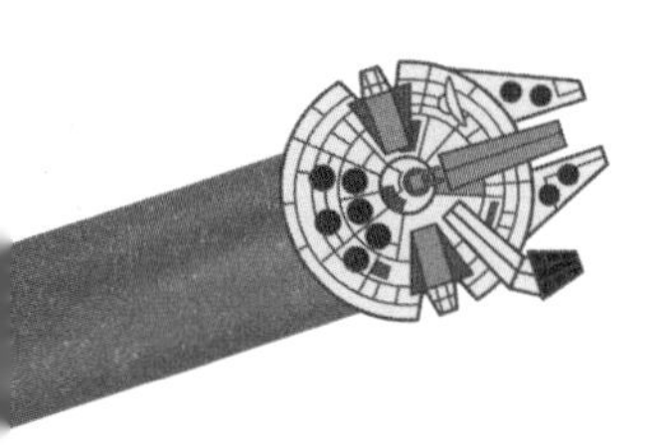

ANAKIN FROWNED. There was no sign of the disturbance both he and Obi-Wan had felt. He tried again, muttering an age-old mantra to center himself.

"There is no emotion; there is peace. There is no ignorance; there is—"

His eyes snapped open. There. He'd felt it . . . in the training stores!

Anakin broke into a run, still gripping the dormant remote in his hand. He turned left and then right, finding the correct door. He barreled into the training store and found . . . nothing.

Dust motes whirled in the dim light, and cluttered shelves rose like cliffs on either side of him.

There was a clank behind him. Anakin turned on his heel, throwing the remote at the figure that lurked in the shadows. The sphere clanged off a beaked head, metal on metal, and laser bolts lanced toward him. Anakin leapt out of the way of the shots, looking up to see three battle droids emerge noisily from their hiding place!

As one, the skeletal robots fired. Anakin leapt up, climbing the shelves as if they were a rock face. He swept out a hand, using the Force to send half a dozen crates tumbling down toward the droids, and rolled onto the now-empty shelf. Bolts slammed into the metal above him as he crawled along the ledge. He needed a weapon, fast.

There were more crates ahead. He opened the first to find blast visors. The next box was more useful; electroblades were neatly stacked within. Another training weapon, the tapered blades could deliver a nasty shock. Anakin had no idea how they'd fare against a droid, but he didn't have any better options.

Snatching two blades from the box, he rolled over the edge of the shelf, dropping to his feet between the droids. All three tin heads were still operational, although Anakin was pleased to see that the falling crates had damaged at least one of the droids. It was missing an arm, wires hanging from the shoulder joint—not that the damage made it any less dangerous. The one-armed clanker raised its weapon, but Anakin brought an electroblade around, striking the robot's wrist. The blow was enough to deflect its aim, the shot going wide. Before it could recover, Anakin rammed the other sword beneath the droid's chest unit. The robot emitted a shrill mechanical screech and clattered onto its back, smoke rising from its servos.

There was no time to celebrate as the droids

on either side of him turned and fired. Anakin somersaulted into the air, the droids taking each other out before he landed back on his feet.

Perhaps Obi-Wan had been right. "Who needs a lightsaber, eh?"

The answer came as more shots streamed through the stacks. Five more droids were advancing toward him, rifles blazing.

Anakin tried to block the shots with the electroblades, but the training weapons were no match for so many blasters. He pushed out with the Force, knocking the droids over like hyperpins, but he knew he couldn't hold them back for long. He dropped into a roll, snatching up a discarded blaster to take out one of his attackers. He turned the weapon on the next droid, but the robot fired first, blasting the rifle from his hands. In desperation, he reached up with the Force, attempting to topple one of the gigantic shelving units onto his assailants, but it was too heavy.

"Anakin—catch!"

He'd never been so happy to hear Obi-Wan's voice. He turned to see a lightsaber spinning toward him—*his* lightsaber. He ignited the blade as soon as it was safely back in his hand. That was more like it. Obi-Wan ran up to him, his own saber flashing, the Temple Guards close behind.

"I thought I told you to stay upstairs."

"And I ignored you," Anakin replied, slicing a droid in two. "I assumed this was another test."

"Less talking and more fighting," one of the guards barked, removing another droid's head with his double-bladed lightsaber pike. Anakin rushed forward . . . but stumbled as a wave of dizziness swept over him. The world shifted around him . . . the narrow confines of the storeroom suddenly replaced by a nightmarish vision of the Jedi Council Chamber, high in the Council spire. The panoramic windows were cracked, the Council members' chairs scattered across the polished floor. He heard blaster fire . . . a scream, and–

"Anakin, look out!"

A lightsaber flashed in front of Anakin's face, blocking the blaster bolt that had nearly taken off his head.

"What's wrong with you?" Obi-Wan snapped, deflecting a flurry of plasma shots.

Anakin was still struggling to stand. "Didn't you feel it?"

"Feel what?"

"The Force . . . it showed me . . . something terrible."

Obi-Wan used the Force to drag a droid toward him, then speared it with his blade. "I don't feel anything."

"I have to go."

“Where?”

“The Council Chamber. Something’s wrong.”

“Something is wrong *here*, in case you haven’t noticed.”

“I can help,” Anakin insisted, turning to leave.

“No,” Obi-Wan said. “We’ll head to the chamber together as soon as we’ve dealt with these blasted droids.”

DOES ANAKIN OBEY OBI-WAN’S COMMAND?

YES—TURN TO PAGE 20.

NO—GO TO PAGE 5.

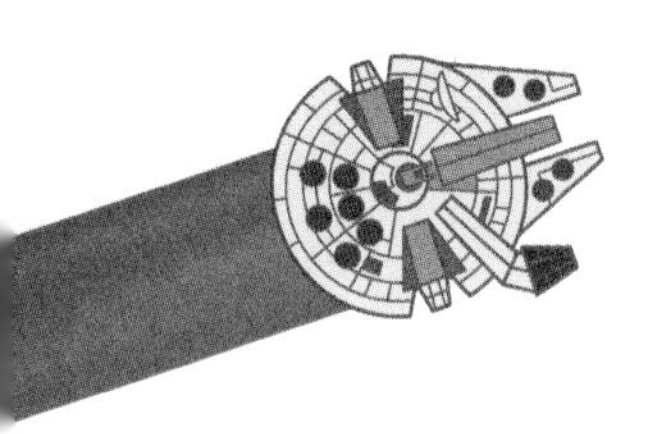

"ANAKIN, CAN YOU HEAR ME?"

Anakin groaned. His head throbbed, and his throat felt as if he'd swallowed a sandstorm. Opening his eyes, he looked into Obi-Wan's face.

"M-Master Yoda. He was—"

"Attacked. Yes, we know. Why didn't you do something?"

"Yoda told me to stay back."

"And you *listened* to him?"

Anakin pushed weakly against Obi-Wan. "You always tell me to do as I'm told."

"You could have saved him, Anakin."

"And you could have come with me!" Anakin snapped, using the floor to push himself up. "You always think you know best. It's not fair."

"Oh, grow up, Anakin," Obi-Wan said before he was interrupted by a voice behind them.

"You *both* need to grow up."

They turned to see a hologram of Mace Windu glaring at them. "Look at you—master and apprentice squabbling like younglings!"

Anakin could barely stay on his feet. "It's Obi-Wan's fault, not mine."

"Oh, very mature," Obi-Wan countered, turning to the hologram. "Do you see what I have to work with?"

"What I see," Mace Windu said icily, "is that Master Yoda has been kidnapped."

Anakin's chin dropped. "I'm sorry."

"As am I, Skywalker," the Jedi Master replied. "I am sorry that neither of you are ready for an investigation of this magnitude. Maybe we wouldn't be in this mess if you had worked together."

Obi-Wan stepped forward. "But—"

"But nothing. You are dismissed. Both of you."

Anakin didn't know what was worse—that he could barely walk as he stumbled out of the chamber or the look on Obi-Wan's face as he stalked toward the turbolift in disgrace.

THE END

CAN YOU HELP ANAKIN AND OBI-WAN MAKE BETTER CHOICES?

THERE WAS A CLATTER in the room to his right. They were in the linen stores!

Sliding open the door, Anakin crept between the towering shelves, pausing at a gap between the stacks.

Someone was walking toward him.

He looked around, spotting piles of neatly folded sheets on a nearby shelf. When the intruder was nearly upon him, Anakin used the Force to send the crisp linen flying at the figure. The sheets whirled around the trespasser, wrapping them from head to toe like a Jundland mummy.

"Master, I have them!" Anakin shouted.

A blue lightsaber burst from the fabric, slicing through the linen cocoon. Scorched sheets fell away to reveal an angry-looking Obi-Wan.

"No, Anakin—you have *me*!"

"M-Master!" Anakin stammered. "I'm sorry."

Obi-Wan glared at his Padawan. "I thought I told you to stay upstairs."

"I thought I could help."

Kenobi kicked the singed sheets at his feet. "This is helping?"

Laser fire streaked between them. The two Jedi turned to see a battle droid advancing.

"Give me my lightsaber," Anakin demanded, but Obi-Wan pushed him back.

"I think I can handle one solitary droid," he said.

Something glinted in the droid's hand. Anakin called out a warning just as the battle droid threw a grenade at Obi-Wan's feet. It detonated with a sharp clap, washing them with a blazing light.

"Anakin?" Obi-Wan shouted.

"I can't see," Anakin called back, blinking wildly.

"I think that's rather the point."

Anakin's vision slowly cleared. He looked up to see Obi-Wan rubbing his eyes.

A Temple Guard ran up, lightsaber pike drawn. "What happened?"

"There was a battle droid," Obi-Wan told him. "It set off a flash grenade and vanished."

"Now we'll never know what it was doing here," Anakin complained. "You should have listened to me."

"And you shouldn't have distracted me," Obi-Wan replied. "Come on. The Council will want our report."

THE END

CAN YOU HELP ANAKIN AND OBI-WAN MAKE BETTER CHOICES?

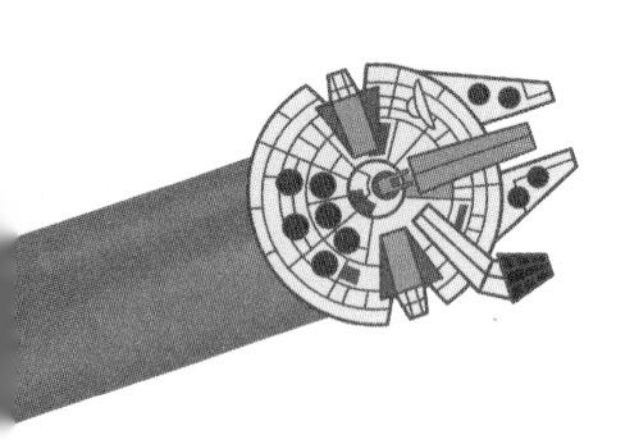

"SORRY," ANAKIN SAID to the immobile guard as he leapt into the turbolift and slammed the controls. He hoped the Jedi was okay, but he needed to keep moving. As the car zoomed up to the top of the spire, Anakin fought back any lingering guilt he felt about the poor guy. If the roles were reversed, the guard would have probably done the same, right?

But all thoughts of the guard vanished as the turbolift doors opened. . . .

Grand Master Yoda was locked in a lightsaber duel, blocking a ferocious attack from a Temple Guard!

The masked traitor lunged with his double-bladed pike, but Yoda somersaulted over the searing weapon to land nimbly on the back of his own chair. The guard pivoted, bringing his pike around, but Yoda shoved forward with the Force, knocking the guard on his back.

"Skywalker," Yoda rasped as he noticed Anakin rushing in to help. "Not your fight this is. Stay back."

DOES ANAKIN DO WHAT YODA COMMANDS?

YES—TURN TO PAGE 12.

NO—GO TO PAGE 22.

ANAKIN'S HAND WENT TO HIS SIDE. Obi-Wan still had his saber. A smile crossed his lips.

Make sure everything's back where it belongs, eh?

He'd better start with his lightsaber.

Obi-Wan had killed the turbolift controls to stop Anakin from following, but there was more than one way to trap a mynock.

Anakin searched behind the large tapestries that hung from the ceilings until he found a metal grate set into the wall. The grate was magna-locked in place, so Anakin used the Force to rip it away, revealing a service duct that was part of a network that ran throughout the entire temple . . . including down to the storage level.

This particular shaft plunged vertically into darkness, a rickety ladder bolted on the other side of the sheer drop. Usually, only maintenance droids traveled those passageways. It was going to be a long climb.

SHOULD ANAKIN USE THE LADDER?

YES—TURN TO PAGE 10.

NO—TURN TO PAGE 13.

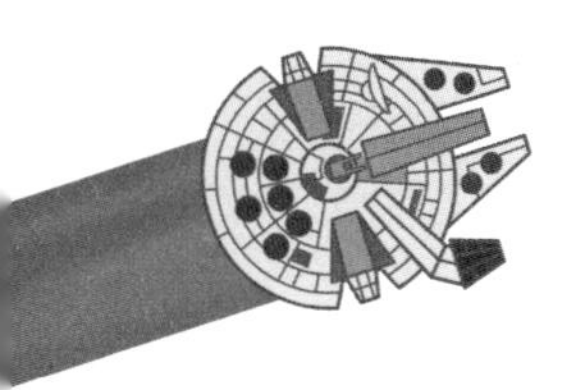

ANAKIN REACTED WITHOUT THINKING, lashing out with his lightsaber.

"I thought I told you to keep a low profile!" Obi-Wan hissed, dragging his Padawan away. Camera droids buzzed around them, transmitting Anakin's image to the giant screens that hovered above the field.

A crowd jeered and surged toward them like an angry mob.

WHAT DO THEY DO?

RUN—TURN TO PAGE 52.

FIGHT—GO TO PAGE 61.

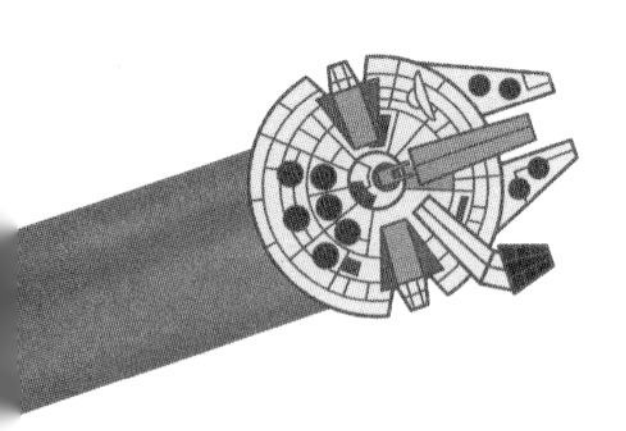

"DON'T WORRY," Anakin said, glancing around. "I'll blend right in."

"That *would* make a pleasant change," Obi-Wan said as Anakin started toward a large archway. "Now where are you going?"

"To the market," Anakin said, beckoning for him to follow. "Watto always told me, 'You wanna find out what's happening, hang around with stall holders. They're the biggest gossips this side of the whispering nebula.'"

Obi-Wan smiled at Anakin's impression of his former master. "I'll take his word for it. Personally, I've always favored a nice cozy cantina."

The Jedi stepped beneath the arch and found themselves in a bustling covered market, stalls packed tight on either side selling everything from tangy tea leaves and squirming worm noodles to snapping barghests and caged tooka kittens. It was much busier than Anakin had imagined it would be, and he soon found himself bumped and jostled by shoppers eager to snare a bargain.

Perhaps the market hadn't been such a good idea.

They could barely move, let alone ask around about Sanberge.

A tiny droid bumped into Anakin, apologizing in a language he didn't understand. He felt the Force prickle even as the robot broke into a run clutching a familiar-looking tool in its pincers. Anakin's hand went to his pouch. That was his bit driver!

"Hey!" he cried out. "Stop, thief!"

"Anakin," Obi-Wan said, gripping his arm. "Let it go. Remember, we don't want to cause a scene."

SHOULD ANAKIN CHASE THE DROID?

YES—GO TO PAGE 56.

NO—TURN TO PAGE 62.

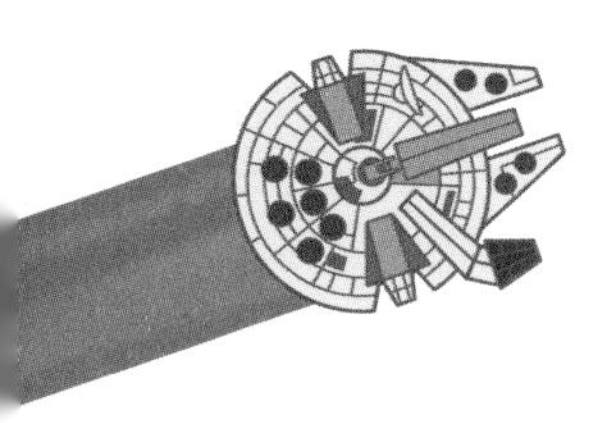

"THERE'S TOO MANY OF THEM!" Obi-Wan shouted as a flying droid appeared in front of the viewport and unloaded its blasters into the transparisteel. "We should surrender."

"No, Master—we can escape."

Obi-Wan shook his head. "Not this time."

Anakin powered down the weapons system. "It was your idea to come here."

"You don't have to remind me," Obi-Wan said as the droids guided them to a floating city.

They were marched at blaster point to face a furious Skakoan administrator. The sulfide breather's wrinkled lips drew back in a toothless snarl.

"What is the meaning of this? Sneaking into our atmosphere? Destroying our droids?"

"They fired on us!" Anakin argued.

"We came because of this," Obi-Wan said, revealing the droid head he'd brought from the temple.

The Skakoan took the metal skull. "A battle droid?"

"One of yours. It attacked the Jedi Temple."

"That's a serious accusation." The administrator passed the head to his assistant. "Check its serial code."

The assistant reported that the droid belonged to a batch stolen by Chagrian smugglers two years previous.

"A batch subsequently recovered by the Jedi," the administrator recalled. "We petitioned the Jedi Council for their return but were told that they were now the property of the Republic. I don't know what game you're playing, Jedi, but we won't stand for it."

Anakin tensed as his arms were grabbed by grasping droids, his lightsaber snatched from his side.

"What will you do with us?" Obi-Wan demanded.

"You will be transported to a prison on the surface," the administrator told them. "In the meantime, I will send word to our representative in the Senate. The Chancellor himself will hear of this."

Anakin leaned over conspiratorially as they were led away. "Don't worry, Master. The Chancellor won't abandon us to the Techno Union."

"Oh, I have every faith in Chancellor Palpatine. I just wish I hadn't wasted our time. Maybe we should have examined those droids more closely, after all. . . ."

THE END

CAN YOU HELP OBI-WAN AND ANAKIN MAKE BETTER CHOICES?

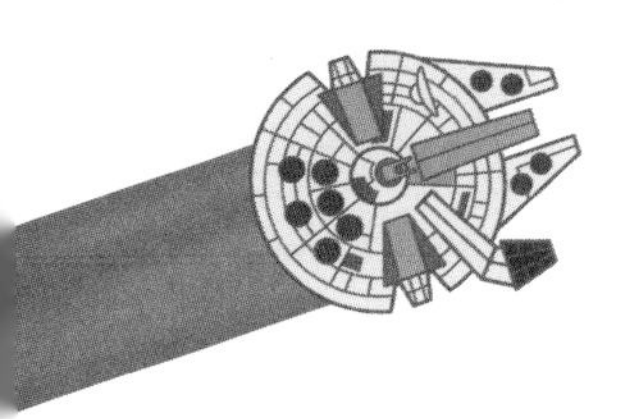

THERE WAS NO WAY they'd win a fight, not in such a crowded place. There was only one thing for it.

"Jump!" Obi-Wan yelled, springing into the air.

Anakin followed, using the Force to leap over the Klatooinians' lumpy heads.

The Jedi hopscotched from stall to stall until they reached an exit.

Behind them, they could hear the Hutt barking orders, but at least the Klatoonians would never get through that crowd.

"So much for markets," Obi-Wan said, adjusting his hood.

"Have you got any better ideas?" Anakin asked, checking that the bit driver was still in its pouch.

GO TO PAGE 76.

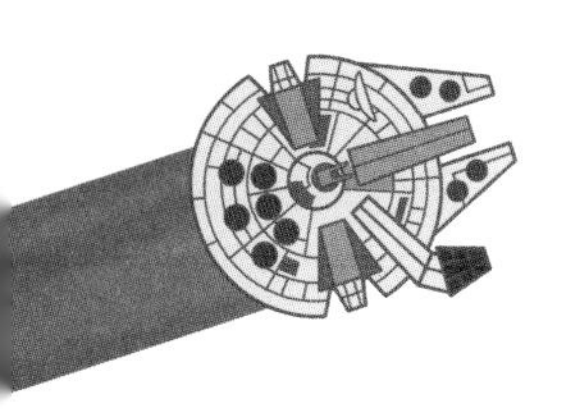

“WE SHOULD EXAMINE the holofeeds,” Obi-Wan suggested, accessing a control on a nearby chair. A cluster of holoscreens appeared, each displaying a different part of the temple. There were rooms from all five spires, plus various hangars, workshops, reading rooms, and archives.

Anakin spotted the problem immediately. “They’re frozen. All of them.”

Obi-Wan pressed buttons, trying to rewind the footage, but Anakin was right. Unbelievable as it sounded, someone had hacked the temple’s security system.

“Now what?” Anakin asked.

“We could interview the Temple Guards?”

“That’ll just waste time. We have a perfect clue already—the battle droids!”

WHAT’S THE NEXT STEP IN THEIR INVESTIGATION?

INTERVIEW THE GUARDS—TURN TO PAGE 55.

EXAMINE THE DROIDS—GO TO PAGE 90.

IT WAS EASY TO SEE HOW the Wheel got its name. Anakin had never seen such a large space station, its central ring the diameter of a small moon. The entire structure revolved on a bulbous axis, and lights glittered from a thousand portholes.

"That's . . . incredible," he gasped.

"Stop gawking, Anakin," Obi-Wan murmured. "You look like a tourist."

"We're *supposed* to be tourists," Anakin reminded him. Obi-Wan had insisted that they leave their distinctive Jedi shuttle on a nearby planetoid, booking passage to Besh Gorgon on public transport. An uneasy truce existed between the Republic and Jaspara, the Wheel's current baron administrator. In an attempt to keep the peace, the Jedi had promised not to set foot inside the administrator's dubious establishment.

However, its less-than-respectable reputation seemed to draw large crowds. The hyperbus was packed with pleasure-seekers eager to take advantage of the Wheel's many casinos, sporting arenas, and shopping malls. For all his enthusiasm, Anakin kept his cloak drawn tightly around him as he and Obi-Wan

disembarked. There were folks from all walks of life there, from high nobles to scruffy dockworkers, all ready to squander their credits.

"How are we going to find the mobster?" Anakin shouted, struggling to make himself heard over the crowd as they walked the station's crowded promenade.

"Keep your voice down," Obi-Wan hissed. "We don't want to draw attention to ourselves."

WHERE SHOULD THEY GO?

A CANTINA—GO TO PAGE 76.

A MARKETPLACE—TURN TO PAGE 44.

"RUN!" OBI-WAN YELLED.

"Where?" Anakin asked, looking around. Angry shockball fans were blocking every exit.

Obi-Wan leapt onto the field, and Anakin jumped after him seconds later. They landed just as a player was knocked unconscious by a shockball strike.

"And they call this a sport?" Obi-Wan shouted, narrowly avoiding the electrified ball that whizzed past his head.

"Get off the field!" an armored defender yelled, making a grab for them.

"Gladly!" Obi-Wan said, sidestepping the lumbering brute only to be tackled to the ground by one of his teammates.

Anakin yanked the player from his master's back so Obi-Wan could scramble back to his feet.

"Over there," Obi-Wan said, pointing to a tunnel that presumably led to the team's changing rooms. They raced across the field, dodging angry players and ignoring the jeers from the crowd. Anakin spotted the ball zipping toward them and used the Force to send it bouncing from one player to another, knocking each of them senseless. Anakin raced for the tunnel just as the ball struck him on the side of the head.

It was like being hit by a charging dewback. A cheer went up around the arena as electricity surged through Anakin's body, his legs buckling beneath him.

He hated this game.

THE END

CAN YOU HELP ANAKIN MAKE BETTER CHOICES?

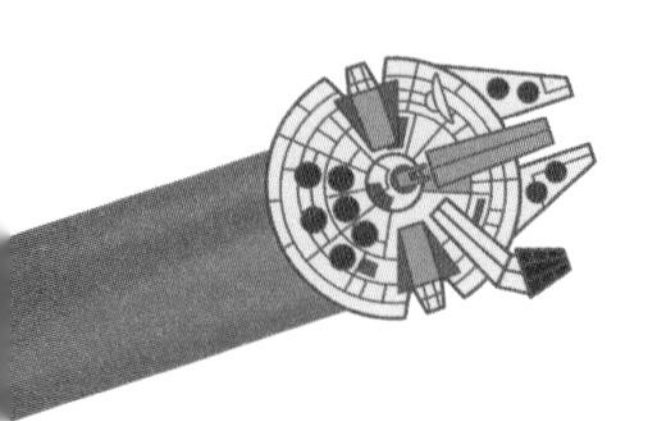

THEY WERE DRAGGED in front of the Wheel's baron administrator, a white-haired Ryn who stared at them as if they'd crawled out of a happabore dung heap.

"Jedi, on the Wheel . . ." Jaspara said, his long tail flicking with disapproval. "How disappointing."

"Just let us go," Anakin wheezed.

"I don't think so," the gray-skinned alien said, his thin lips breaking into a cruel grin. "You will be ransomed back to Coruscant . . . for the right price, of course!"

THE END

CAN YOU HELP ANAKIN AND OBI-WAN MAKE BETTER CHOICES?

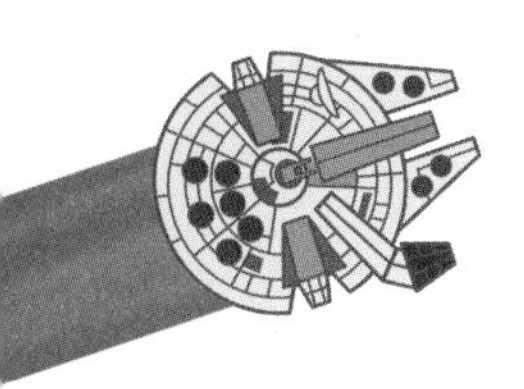

"WHAT DID I TELL YOU?" Anakin groaned as they finished the interviews.

Obi-Wan ran his fingers through his hair. "I thought at least one of them would know something."

"Apparently not."

"Which leaves us with your droids," Obi-Wan admitted, making for the archives where Mace had ordered the droids to be taken.

But when they got there, the archivists couldn't find the droids anywhere. Eventually, Anakin checked the temple's central computer log and discovered they'd been accidentally thrown in a trash compactor.

The trail had gone cold. Master Yoda was missing, and they had no way to find out who'd taken him.

THE END

CAN YOU HELP OBI-WAN AND ANAKIN MAKE BETTER CHOICES?

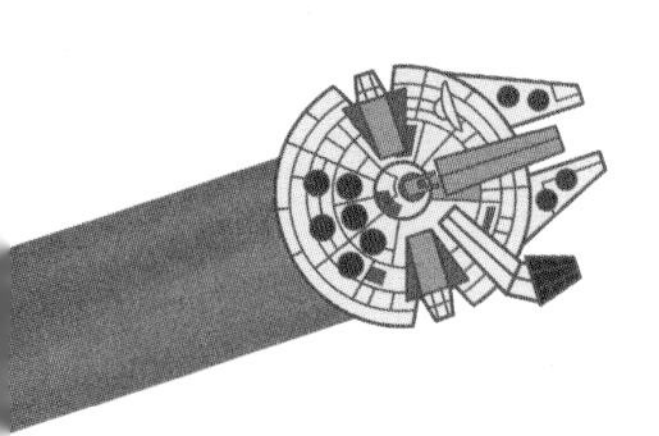

"AS IF I WOULD let anything go," Anakin said, pulling away. He tried to run after the droid but couldn't get past a large Hutt who was haggling with a trader over an aquarium of live paddy frogs.

Anakin wasn't about to give up. He extended an arm, and the light-fingered droid shot up in the air, lifted by the Force. It squealed and twisted, dropping the bit driver, which zipped back to Anakin's open hand.

Smiling, Anakin released the droid, and it clattered to the ground to scuttle away.

"Anakin," Obi-Wan said, pulled his apprentice away from the Hutt, who was eyeing them suspiciously. "What did I say about using the Force?"

"You worry too much," Anakin said, pocketing his tool. "No one noticed. They're all too busy bartering."

But he was wrong.

"Jeedai!" the Hutt bellowed, pointing at them with a stubby finger.

Obi-Wan backed away slowly. "My Huttese is a little rusty," he admitted, "but doesn't that mean . . . ?"

"Jedi!" snarled a Klatooinian, blocking their escape.

Obi-Wan and Anakin turned to find themselves surrounded by a pack of the towering aliens, all clutching vicious-looking staffs and axes.

"Friends of yours?" Obi-Wan asked the Hutt as the Klatooinians closed in.

SHOULD OBI-WAN AND ANAKIN FIGHT THE KLATOOINIANS?

YES—GO TO PAGE 64.

NO—TURN TO PAGE 48.

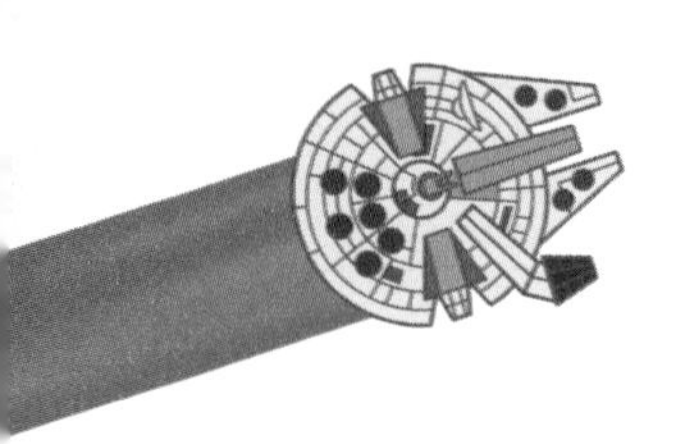

"VERY WELL," Obi-Wan said. "We'll investigate the markings, but if it proves a dead end . . ."

"I'll fly you to Skako myself," Anakin said with a smile.

Obi-Wan's face blanched. "Then let's hope it's a journey that proves unnecessary."

Soon they were standing in the Jedi Archives, waiting as Chief Librarian Jocasta Nu cross-referenced the droid's strange symbols with her beloved records.

"Here we are," the elderly Jedi said as a hologram fizzed to life.

"That's it," Anakin said. "Two diamonds and a star."

"A nine-pointed star," Nu corrected him, "the symbol of the Nova Crime Syndicate."

"I can't say I've heard of them," Obi-Wan said.

Nu chuckled. "Hardly surprising. Nova is no Black Sun." Her nimble fingers danced over the keyboard as if playing a valachord. "They operate out of space station BDT-0978 in the Besh Gorgon system."

"Commonly known as the Wheel," Obi-Wan said, groaning. "A notorious den of crime and depravity if ever I've seen one."

"Sounds like fun," Anakin said with a grin.

Obi-Wan rolled his eyes. "You worry me sometimes."

"Only sometimes?" Anakin said as another hologram formed. "I'll try harder."

They were looking at an angular mask, its face dominated by a V-shaped beak. "Who's this?"

"Grynask Sanberge," Nu told him. "The head of the Nova gang."

"An Anomid," Obi-Wan noted.

"A fascinating species," Nu confirmed. "Possessing no vocal chords, they communicate through a complicated system of facial expressions and hand signals."

"Then how will we understand them?" Anakin asked.

"Oh, it's easier than you think," Obi-Wan said. "An Anomid once served on the Council. He wore a vocoder to translate his facial expressions into Basic."

"Ah, yes," Nu said, her eyes sparkling at the memory. "Alxa Kress. He was particularly fond of Rodian theater. He taught Master Windu how to perform the works of Harido Kavila in the native Rodese."

Anakin was boggled by the thought of Mace Windu onstage. "Master Windu used to . . . *act*?"

"The Council's gain was theater's loss," Nu said wistfully.

"Thank you," Obi-Wan said, putting a stop to the librarian's jaunt down memory lane. "That will be all."

Anakin was still laughing as they strode from the Archives. "Seriously, did you ever see Mace perform?"

"It was before my time," Obi-Wan said. "But may I suggest you stay focused, Anakin. Master Yoda is in danger, and we have a mystery to solve."

"On this Wheel of yours?"

"So it appears," Obi-Wan said, guiding him to the temple's hangar bay. "But *I'm* flying."

GO TO PAGE 50.

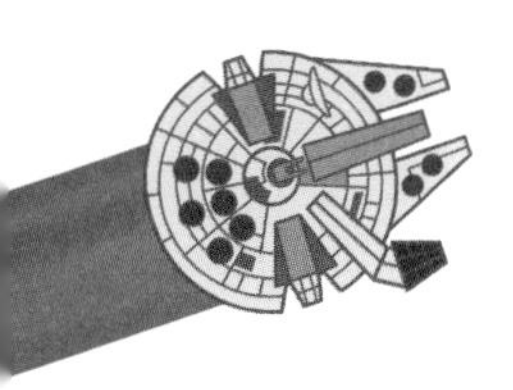

OBI-WAN AND ANAKIN stood back to back, lightsabers blazing. All around them, the crowd pulled out blasters, laser whips, and even vibro-axes.

"Who brings an axe to a ball game?" Anakin said as the mob rushed them.

"Welcome to the Wheel!" Obi-Wan replied, blocking a barrage of blaster bolts.

They were hideously outnumbered but held their ground. They parried and jabbed, kicked and punched, using the Force either to send their aggressors flying into each other or, when all else failed, to rip seats from the stands to use as shields.

But nothing had prepared them for the electrified net that suddenly dropped from above, sparking with the ferocity of a thousand thunder-wasp stings.

Multiarmed security droids rushed forward, barking at them to surrender. As if they had a choice. The Jedi's limbs were like jelly long after the shock net was removed.

TURN TO PAGE 54.

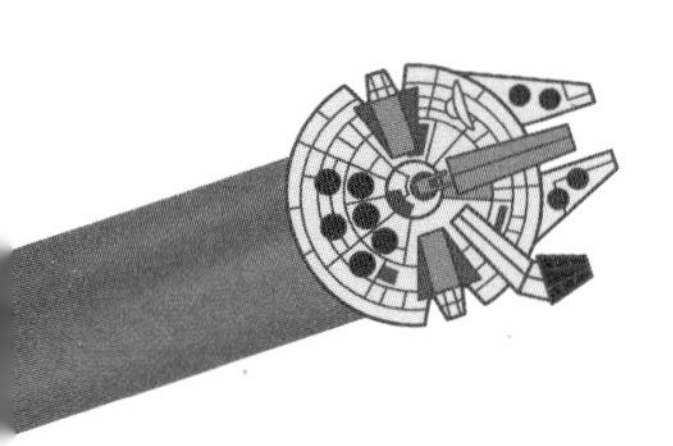

ANAKIN SIGHED. Obi-Wan was right. The marketplace was too crowded. There was no way he could give chase, not without using his powers and revealing that he was a Jedi.

And he should never have listened to Watto. The stall owners were all too busy hustling customers to gossip. It was useless.

"Come on," Obi-Wan said, guiding Anakin to an exit. "Perhaps we should try a cantina after all."

They'd almost made it out of the market when a voice rang out: "Hey, you in the cloak."

Anakin turned to see a four-armed security officer marching toward them, shock batons held in two of his hands. Obi-Wan shot Anakin a worried glance. Had they been discovered?

"Is there a problem, Officer?" the older Jedi asked.

"Is this yours?" the security officer said, holding up Anakin's bit driver.

"Yes!" Anakin exclaimed, taking it back. "A droid stole it from me."

The officer nodded. "I've had my eyes on that little tech-head for a while. . . ." His voice trailed off, his gaze dropping to Anakin's belt. Anakin grimaced, immediately realizing his mistake. He had slipped the bit driver back into its pouch, revealing his lightsaber in the process.

"We can explain . . ." Obi-Wan said, but it was already too late. The shock batons jabbed forward, knocking Obi-Wan and Anakin off their feet.

TURN TO PAGE 54.

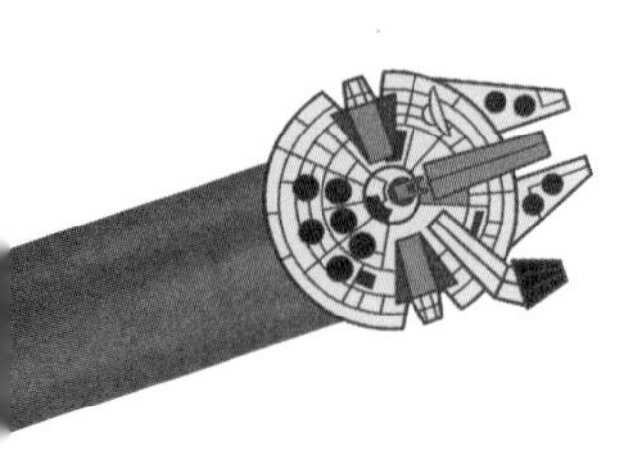

THERE WAS NO POINT pretending any longer. Obi-Wan and Anakin drew their lightsabers, whirling their blades in an attempt to disarm the Klatooinians. It was hopeless. There was barely room to swing a tooka, let alone fight. Anakin sliced through a vibro-club only to have the butt of a rifle thud into the back of his leg. His knee buckled and he pitched forward, his lightsaber dropping from his hand. Obi-Wan didn't fare any better. A Klatooinian shoved a shock stick into the Jedi's side, sending energy cascading down Obi-Wan's legs. The Jedi crumpled to the ground at the exact moment one of the aliens brought a club crashing down into the back of Anakin's head.

Anakin woke in the stinking hull of the Hutt's ship. Groaning, he felt the lump on his skull.

"Maybe the market wasn't such a good idea, Master," he admitted before realizing that Obi-Wan wasn't with him. He looked around to see the Hutt leering at him through an open doorway.

Anakin threw up his hand to grab the disgusting slug with the Force but cried out as electricity surged from the collar he hadn't realized was around his neck.

“I have customers who will pay a good price for Jedi slaves,” the Hutt gurgled before slithering away. “Shame your friend got away.”

Anakin smiled despite the pain from the collar. Obi-Wan had escaped. The Hutt would be laughing on the other side of his slimy face when Anakin’s master burst in to rescue him. Anakin would look forward to that . . . but not the lecture Obi-Wan was sure to give him once they were safely back on Coruscant.

He fingered the slave collar, triggering yet another painful jolt. Anakin was *never* going to live this down.

THE END

CAN YOU HELP ANAKIN MAKE BETTER CHOICES?

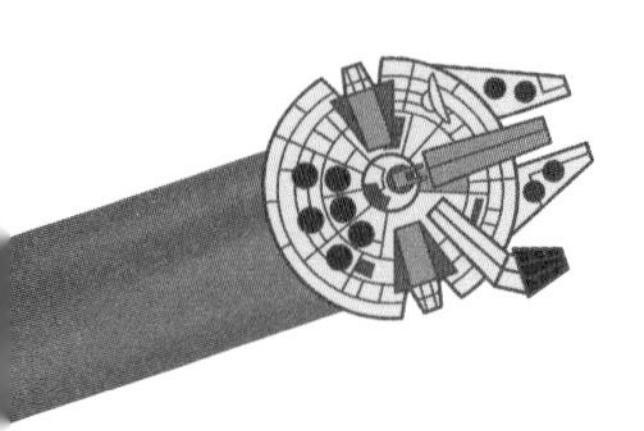

OBI-WAN PLACED a warning hand on Anakin's arm.

"Now, Anakin, there's no need to threaten the poor fellow." He turned to the Anomid. "You want to help, don't you?"

The alien hesitated, shaking his cowled head.

"Your Jedi mind tricks won't work with me," the vocoder rasped.

"You know who we are then, and why we're here?"

Again, the mobster paused before answering. Anakin didn't know if it was the vocoder struggling to translate his facial expressions or Sanberge attempting to resist Obi-Wan's influence.

"I know nothing."

"I sense you possess a strong will," Obi-Wan said, his voice calm and steady. "You can easily resist our . . . what did you call them?"

"Jedi mind tricks," Anakin reminded him.

"Ah, yes. That's right, isn't it, Grynask?"

"That's right," the Anomid replied, a slightly dreamlike slur creeping into the artificial voice.

"You're an intelligent being . . ."

"I'm an intelligent being . . ."

"Who wants to tell us about the droids."

"I want to tell you about the droids."

Obi-Wan and Anakin shared a satisfied smile before the Padawan pressed their advantage.

"Why did you send them to the Jedi Temple?"

"I—I was told to," Sanberge replied. "By the client."

"And who exactly was that?" Obi-Wan asked.

"I can't tell you."

"You *will* tell us," Anakin insisted, but Obi-Wan motioned for him to back off.

"It's not that he won't reveal their identity, Anakin, but that he doesn't know. Isn't that right, Grynask?"

The terrified Anomid nodded.

"Then how did they contact you?" Anakin said. "A hologram?"

"No," the Anomid replied. "Audio only, via a deep-space relay."

"You want to play it for us, don't you?" Obi-Wan suggested.

Obediently, the mobster pressed a button on his wrist comm.

"I require a squadron of battle droids," a tinny voice hissed from the communicator's tiny speakers. *"To be delivered to Coruscant immediately."*

"That voice," Anakin said.

Obi-Wan nodded. "Modulated."

“Like the guard who took Master—”

A warning glance from Obi-Wan told Anakin not to mention Yoda’s name in front of Sanberge.

“You want to give us that comlink,” Obi-Wan said, holding out his hand.

Sanberge nodded, unclipped the unit, and passed it to the Jedi.

“Thank you. You’ve been most helpful.”

Obi-Wan and Anakin turned to leave, and Sanberge rubbed his mask as if waking from a dream.

“Oh, yes,” Obi-Wan said, pausing by the door. “Try an aura petal rub. I hear they’re awfully good for stress.”

They left Sanberge stumbling toward the hot petal treatments, and headed back to the hyperbus terminal.

Safely back on their own shuttle, Anakin connected Sanberge’s comlink to the main computer. He wished R2-D2 was there. His astromech buddy would’ve made short work of decrypting the recording.

“Well?” Obi-Wan asked, peering over his shoulder.

Anakin fed the metadata from the recording through the shuttle’s star maps, tracing the message to its point of origin. A holochart appeared in the air in front of them.

“The Jalor system,” Obi-Wan observed. “Can we narrow it down?”

Anakin shook his head. "According to the data stream, the broadcast could have come from either Melacon, Ramitrix, or Glee Anselm." A thought occurred to him. "However . . ."

He played back the recording.

"I require a squadron of battle droids, to be delivered to Coruscant immediately."

"Did you hear that?"

"No," Obi-Wan admitted.

Anakin played back the second half of the recording.

"There," Anakin said, "behind the voice. It sounds like . . ."

"Water," Obi-Wan realized. "But Melacon is an arid world. . . ."

"And Ramitrix is a lifeless rock," Anakin said, zooming in on a blue planet. "Whereas Glee Anselm . . ."

"Is largely covered in ocean."

Anakin shrugged. "It's not the strongest lead. . . ."

Obi-Wan nodded. "But it's all we have."

GO TO PAGE 118.

ANAKIN GLANCED BACK at the still-smoking droids. That was it! The jet packs!

Kicking the droids apart, he yanked a pack free and strapped it to his back. Without checking to see if it was still operational, he took a running start and launched himself through the shattered window.

He slapped the controls. The jets didn't fire. He tried again, but still there was nothing. Gravity took hold, and he plummeted toward the ground.

The rockets ignited on the third attempt, shooting him up after the freighter. Within seconds, he was in the clouds, but the ship was too far away. Knowing he was pushing the jet pack to its limits, he twisted the speed control, the wind stinging his eyes.

The gap between him and the freighter narrowed. Yes. He was doing it. He could feel the scorching heat of the ship's rockets against his skin, the thunder of its engine drowning out the whine of his own pack. Just a little closer and he'd . . . what? Slice himself through the hull? Sever a fuel line?

He'd have to work it out when he got there.

If he got there.

A cannon swiveled to face him! He'd been spotted. Good. That meant the pilot was rattled. With any luck, they'd start making mistakes.

He ignited his lightsaber just as plasma bolts flashed toward him. The blasts ricocheted off his blade to hit one of the thrusters. The ship slowed, its damaged thruster belching thick smoke. Anakin choked on the fumes as he flew into the black cloud, reaching forward to grab the hull.

He was almost there. . . .

Almost . . .

There . . .

The jet pack spluttered and failed just as Anakin's fingers brushed the ship's plating. He tumbled, bellowing in frustration.

Anakin slapped the pack's control, yelling at it to reengage, but the pack was dead. Clipping his lightsaber to his belt, he struggled with the pack's straps, trying to pull it from his back. Perhaps he could hot-wire the rockets. Instead, the wind snatched the pack from his grip.

Anakin plummeted out of control for the second time in as many hours. Dark spots danced on the edges of his vision. He couldn't black out. He *wouldn't*. The world became a blur—the neon of holographic advertisements, the blare of airspeeder horns, and the roar of the rushing wind melting together as he tumbled to the ground.

The air exploded from his lungs as he jolted to a stop. Anakin opened his eyes and tried to focus. He was still high above the ground, slowly rising as if being lifted by a giant hand. Every part of him ached, but he craned his neck, looking up to see Obi-Wan leaning out of the Council Chamber window, arm outstretched and hair whipping in the wind. His master had saved him and was reeling him in like a glottlefish on a line.

"Master Yoda has been captured . . ." he gasped as

Obi-Wan helped him back through the broken window, "... by a Temple Guard."

"A guard? Are you sure?"

The question came not from Obi-Wan but from a full-size hologram of Mace Windu that flickered into view in the Jedi Master's customary place.

Anakin nodded, still trying to catch his breath. "I couldn't stop him."

"That's hardly surprising," Obi-Wan told him. "Temple Guards are skilled Jedi. I'm sorry I didn't listen to you."

Mace's hologram was pacing the chamber. "The droid attack must have been a diversion."

"So Master Yoda could be taken," Obi-Wan said. "Yes, I'm inclined to agree."

Temple Guards stomped into the chamber, dragging a body. It was the guard Anakin had seen earlier at the foot of the turbolift. They dropped the lifeless form in front of Obi-Wan, the mask falling away to reveal the metallic beak of a battle droid.

"This one was booby-trapped," the guard commander informed them. "Rigged to emit knockout gas if disturbed."

"The handiwork of our traitor, I assume," Obi-Wan said, crouching to examine the droid.

The commander tensed at the accusation. "Whoever took Master Yoda wasn't one of us. All guards are present and correct."

Obi-Wan stroked his beard. "An imposter, then."

"So it appears, sir."

"Which leaves us with one all-important question. . . ."

Anakin nodded. "Just who was beneath that mask?"

HOW WILL THEY FIND OUT?

EXAMINE SECURITY FOOTAGE—GO TO PAGE 49.

EXAMINE THE DROIDS—TURN TO PAGE 90.

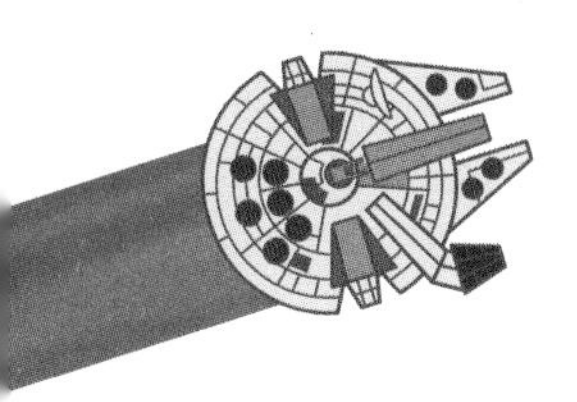

ANAKIN LIMPED OVER to the aft station, hoping that the transmitter was still working. He thumbed the comlink and heard a welcome crackle of static.

"Jedi Temple, we have crashed on Skako Minor. . . ." He glanced at his master, still slumped in his chair. "Obi-Wan has been injured. We need assistance."

"You need to surrender," squawked a mechanical voice.

Anakin sighed as he heard the clank of droids behind him. He swiveled in his chair, blue stun beams already washing over him.

He crashed to the deck, not even knowing if his message had gotten through.

THE END

CAN YOU HELP ANAKIN MAKE BETTER CHOICES?

THE OLDER JEDI TURNED, spotting something on the other side of the promenade. "Ah, that looks like just the ticket. Are you thirsty, Anakin?"

Anakin followed his gaze and saw Obi-Wan was looking at a gaudy cantina, its name picked out in neon Twi'leki—the Cosmo Lounge. Minutes later, they were sitting in a plush booth, "enjoying" the warbling of a tone-deaf Hutt singer.

Obi-Wan beckoned a service droid and asked for two mupple juices and information. Within seconds, crystal goblets had been placed in front of them and a squat Ortolan scurried over to their table, large ears flopping around his pudgy head.

"You drinkin' that?" the Ortolan asked, pointing at Obi-Wan's glass with his trunk. Obi-Wan pushed the goblet over to the blubbery alien, who dipped a stubby toe into the glass and sucked the pink juice noisily through it.

The velvet-skinned alien sighed with satisfaction as he finished the drink. "That's better. Sellin' secrets sure is thirsty work."

“I’m glad we could help,” Obi-Wan told him. “Perhaps you can return the favor.”

“Depends.”

“On what?” Anakin asked.

Obi-Wan produced a pile of credits from his robes and placed them in front of the informant.

“On that,” the Ortolan said. “Triss Terasu, at yer service. What you lookin’ for?”

“Not what?” Anakin said, leaning across the table. “*Who*. A lowlife by the name of Grynask Sanberge.”

Triss rubbed his trunk. “Not sure I’ve heard the name.”

“And what will prompt your memory?” Obi-Wan asked with a knowing smile. “More credits?”

“We’ve already paid him!” Anakin complained.

Obi-Wan raised a hand. “Now, Anakin. There is no need to cause a scene. Mr. Terasu wants to help us, don’t you?”

Triss’s already flabby expression went slack. “I wanna help ya.”

“You can tell us where to find Sanberge.”

“I can tell ya where to find Sanberge,” the Ortolan repeated blankly.

“Well?” Anakin prompted.

Triss shook his head as if waking from a daydream.

"What? Hey, I've had enough of this," he said, glaring at them. "From what I've heard, Sanberge loves his shockball. There's a game today in the Ashton Stadium on the third level. Just follow the sound of a baying crowd, okay?"

Fortunately, it didn't take them long to find the stadium. The match was already in full swing. The rules seemed simple enough: Two teams threw an electrified ball at each other. Whoever got hit would be knocked unconscious. The team with the most players still on their feet at the final whistle was crowned champion.

A quick glance at the field revealed that Jaspara's team—the Galactic Globetrotters—was thrashing the visitors, a lackluster bunch called the Ballistic Banthas. Most of the Banthas' players were already spread-eagle on the synthi-turf, the Globetrotters' fans cheering with every strike.

Obi-Wan had bought tickets for the home stand, gambling that Sanberge would support the local side. His hunch paid off. They soon spotted the Anomid gesticulating widely as yet another Bantha was knocked senseless.

Sanberge turned at the wrong moment and saw them pointing in his direction. He jumped up from his seat, barging over a long-eared Lepi who was yelling at the referee droid.

"He's getting away!" Anakin cried out, vaulting over a row of seats. In his haste, he slammed into a hulking Whiphid, knocking a bag of sticky doughnuts from his huge, hairy hands.

The shaggy alien reared up, furious that Anakin had spilled his shockball snack.

HOW SHOULD ANAKIN DEAL WITH THE RILED WHIPHID?

USE HIS LIGHTSABER—TURN TO PAGE 43.

USE THE FORCE—GO TO PAGE 83.

OBI-WAN WON THE ARGUMENT. Anakin tried to put his case forward, but Mace sided with his fellow Jedi.

Anakin brooded all the way to Skako Minor. Even as they dipped into the planet's atmosphere, Anakin was trying to persuade Obi-Wan that they should return to Coruscant.

"If this is a dead end . . ."

"Anakin, please. We need to concentrate. If we're picked up by the Techno Union's sensor net . . ."

Anakin sighed. “It’s too late for that. We’re being followed.”

Obi-Wan activated a screen, revealing the yellow sky behind the shuttle.

“Are those birds?”

Anakin pressed a control, and the picture zoomed in. “No. Battle droids.”

Obi-Wan’s shoulders sagged. “They can fly now?”

The droids had almost caught up with them, orange wings spread wide. They were sleeker than standard

B1s, with knife-thin heads and fins on their legs guiding their flight. They swarmed the shuttle, integrated blasters already firing.

WHAT SHOULD ANAKIN AND OBI-WAN DO?

ESCAPE—GO TO PAGE 88.

SURRENDER—TURN TO PAGE 46.

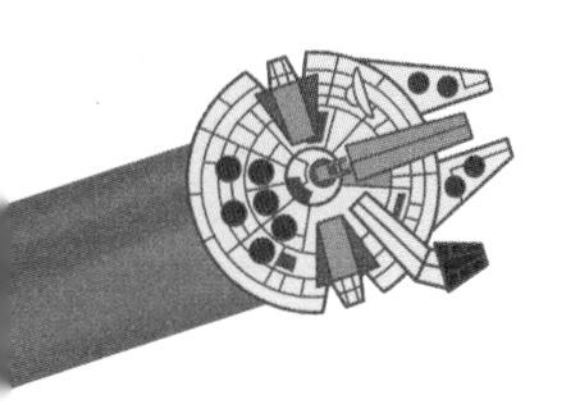

"MY FRIEND DIDN'T MEAN any harm," Obi-Wan said. "Let me buy you another bag."

The lumbering brute roared in response, swiping at Obi-Wan with a hairy hand. The blow sent Obi-Wan crashing into a doughnut dispenser droid nearby.

The Whiphid wheeled on Anakin, saliva dripping from his cracked tusks. Anakin went for his lightsaber but remembered Obi-Wan's warning about the Jedi pact. Instead, he called on the Force and reached out toward the dispenser droid. The droid murmured a worried "Oh, no" as its chrome-plated head flipped open and warm doughnuts shot everywhere. The Whiphid bawled as the sticky treats gummed up his fur and stuck to his craggy face. All around, hungry spectators scrabbled for a free snack.

Obi-Wan scrambled to his feet and joined Anakin in running for the exit. They barreled out of the arena, spotting the Lepi whom Sanberge had knocked over.

"What happened to the Anomid?" Obi-Wan asked the disgruntled shockball fan.

"That creep? He went that way," the bucktoothed Lepi sneered, pointing at a nearby ultraspa.

Sure enough, Sanberge was disappearing through a pair of luxurious sliding doors. The Jedi charged after him, running into a lavish waiting room, but there was no one to be seen except for a Gungan receptionist who bustled toward them.

"Can mesa help, gentlemen? A relaxing sonic massage perhaps? Or a hot mud treatment?"

"No, thank you," Obi-Wan said, eager to be spared the sales patter.

"Yousa sure?" the Gungan said, undaunted. "Da mud is fresh from Mimban, rich in hyperbaride deposits. . . ."

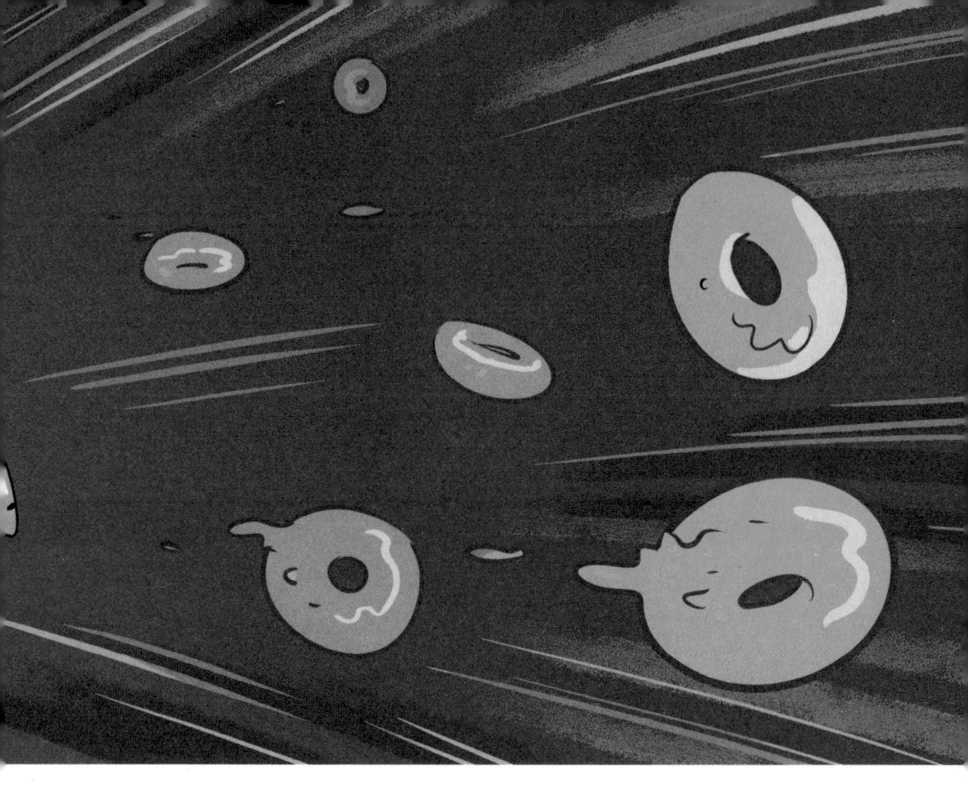

“We’re looking for our . . . friend,” Anakin said. “An Anomid. We thought he came in here.”

“Yeah, yeah,” the Gungan replied, wringing her hands. “Hesa skedaddled straight for da changing rooms. Hesa look berry tense. Mesa suggest an aura petal rub to ease his troubles away.”

“We’ll be sure to mention it,” Obi-Wan told her as they ran through the changing room doors.

The room was empty, save for a Gamorrean wrapped in a large fluffy towel.

“Apologies for barging in,” Obi-Wan said, but the

Gamorrean just grunted and trudged off to the mud baths.

Both Jedi reached out with their senses, drawn instantly to a door near the turboshowers. They approached cautiously before pressing the control. The door slid back to reveal a closet full of recharging janitor droids . . . and Grynask Sanberge, a scatter blaster in hand.

The mobster fired, but Anakin had already drawn his lightsaber to deflect the shot. Sanberge cried out as Anakin sliced straight through his stubby weapon. The ruined blaster tumbled to the floor, and Sanberge cradled his fingers.

"Don't hurt me," he whimpered through his vocoder mask, the artificial voice wavering.

"We just want to chat," Obi-Wan said.

"I-I've nothing to say to you," Sanberge said, backing farther into the closet.

"Are you sure about that?" Anakin said, stepping in after him.

HOW DO THEY MAKE SANBERGE TALK?

ANAKIN INTIMIDATES HIM—TURN TO PAGE 92.

A JEDI MIND TRICK—GO TO PAGE 66.

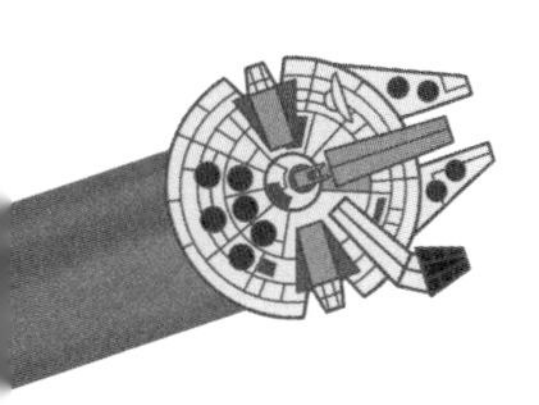

ANAKIN HAULED OBI-WAN through the forest of giant mushrooms. He had to get them away from the ship. There was no way of knowing the extent of the damage. All it would take was one ruptured fuel line. . . .

His feet slipped on the carpet of slick moss, and he thudded to the ground, pain shooting through his damaged shoulder as Obi-Wan landed on top of him. Anakin tried to move, but the Jedi was dead weight. He closed his eyes, exhausted.

Something sharp brushed his face. He looked up to see a tall tribesman holding a spear that rested on Anakin's cheek. He and Obi-Wan were surrounded by purple-skinned aliens. They were lean but muscular, with bulging eyes and sharklike teeth.

Anakin's head felt as if it was stuffed with bantha wool. He couldn't even fight back as he and Obi-Wan were dragged back to the aliens' village. Why hadn't Obi-Wan listened to him on Coruscant?

THE END

CAN YOU HELP ANAKIN MAKE BETTER CHOICES?

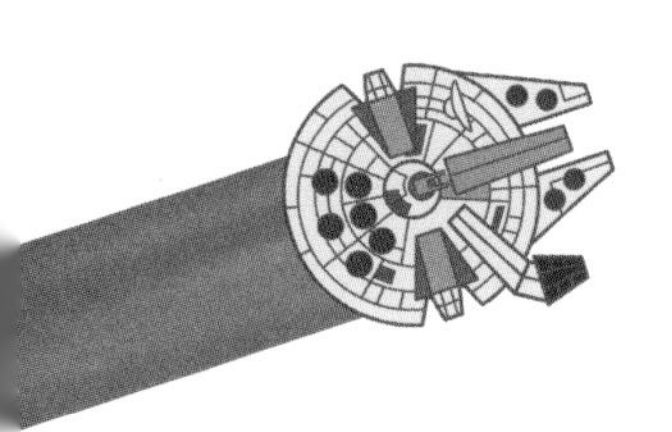

“THERE’S TOO MANY of them!” Obi-Wan shouted as a flying droid appeared in front of the viewport and unloaded its blasters into the transparisteel.

“Hold on!” Anakin said, throwing the ship into a dive.

“Are you *trying* to crash?”

“No,” Anakin said, pulling up sharply again. “I’m trying to lose them.”

“Well you’re not doing a very good job!”

An explosion reverberated through the ship.

“Oh, no,” Anakin muttered, rattling the controls.

“Oh, no, what?”

“They’ve knocked out the main drive.” The shuttle pitched downward, rushing toward the ground. “This time we really *are* crashing!”

“We should eject,” Obi-Wan said, groping for the release at the base of his seat. “One.”

“Two,” Anakin said, grabbing his own lever.

“Three!”

They both pulled . . . and nothing happened. The mechanism had jammed.

The shuttle plowed into the ground.

• • •

Anakin coughed violently as he came to. A pungent yellow mist was rolling into the cockpit, reeking of rotten eggs.

"Hydrogen sulfide," he croaked, holding his breath as he pulled breathers from an overhead compartment. Everything hurt, but he couldn't give up. Obi-Wan was slumped in his chair, head lolled forward. The Jedi was badly hurt.

Anakin slipped a breather over Obi-Wan's head. "Don't worry, Master. I'll get us to safety, one way or another."

SHOULD THEY STAY IN THE SHUTTLE?

YES—TURN TO PAGE 75.

NO—GO TO PAGE 87.

ANAKIN KNELT BESIDE the defeated droids. "Maybe these guys can help."

He picked up a severed droid head and used his bit driver to pry open the faceplate, crinkling his nose as an acrid stench wafted from a mass of charred circuitry.

"This makes no sense. The receptors are fused."

"Damage from your lightsaber?" Obi-Wan asked.

Anakin shook his head. "More like a fail-safe in case the droids were destroyed."

"Deactivated droids tell no tales."

Anakin probed the robot's transmission lines, lifting a knot of charred cables. "At least we know who made them."

Obi-Wan peered closer. "How?"

Anakin tapped a cluster of receivers. "The signal confirmation module. It's a type used by the Techno Union. See?"

Obi-Wan stood and turned to Mace Windu's hologram. "We should approach the Techno Union's representative on the Senate."

The hologram raised a flickering eyebrow. "Gume Saam? He's no fan of the Jedi."

“Then we go straight to the source,” Obi-Wan said, “the union’s headquarters on Skako Minor.”

“We might not have to,” Anakin said, still examining the droid.

“What have you spotted?” Mace Windu asked.

Anakin stood, showing them the faceplate. “This symbol,” he said, pointing to a faint green sigil printed between the optical sensors. “That’s not the Techno Union’s logo. It’s not even their colors.”

“You said it yourself,” Obi-Wan insisted. “The droids are theirs.”

“They made them, yes, but can we really be sure they were behind the attack?”

WHAT SHOULD THEY DO NEXT?

INVESTIGATE THE STRANGE MARKINGS ON THE DROIDS—GO TO PAGE 58.

GO TO SKAKO MINOR—TURN TO PAGE 80.

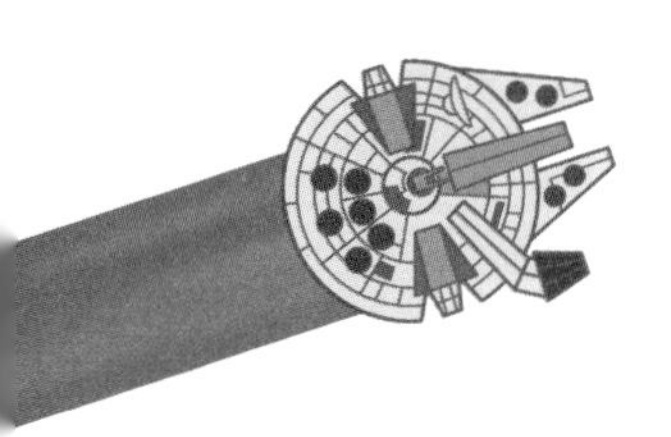

"LEAVE ME ALONE," the Anomid bleated. Anakin could feel the alien's fear as his lightsaber burst to life, the blade's thrum louder than ever in the cramped closet.

"We will—once you've told us what we want to know . . . or lost an arm. Your choice."

"Anakin!" Obi-Wan warned, but Anakin didn't listen.

"Perhaps that's the real reason the Jedi aren't welcome on the Wheel. People like you think you know power, but you have no idea."

"I know a bully when I see one," Sanberge rasped, pressing a button on his sleeve.

A siren blared, red lights strobing all around.

"You little worm," Anakin snarled, but Obi-Wan grabbed his arm before he could make good on his earlier threat.

"Anakin, we need to get out of here. This is not the way."

It was too late. Security droids streamed into the changing room, their telescopic arms bristling with snapping pincers and glowing beam emitters.

“You will surrender,” they barked as one.

“No, we won’t,” Anakin said, raising his lightsaber only to be disarmed, the hilt swatted from his hand by an unseen force.

He turned on Obi-Wan, who stood facing him, palm raised.

“Why did you do *that*?”

“This is a battle we cannot win,” Obi-Wan said, surrendering to the droids. “Fight and we bring the Order into disrepute.”

Anakin couldn’t believe what he was hearing. “We can’t just give up!” he yelled as the droids dragged them away.

“We can, and we will. Prisoners have rights, even here. We will message the Council, asking for their help. Diplomacy will save us, not violence.”

THE END

CAN YOU HELP ANAKIN MAKE BETTER CHOICES?

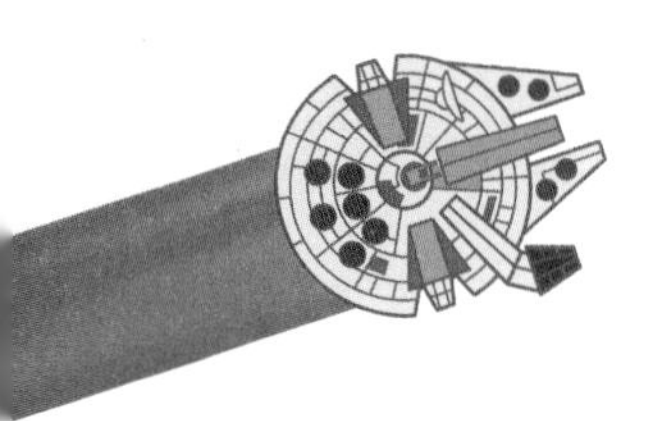

"SUPERSTITIOUS, YOU SAY?"

Anakin had an idea.

He closed his eyes and concentrated, the ground beneath his feet starting to quake. He felt the Force flowing through him.

Soil tumbled from the pit's walls, and Anakin rose to hover majestically above the Anselmi, who dropped to their knees in terror.

"Your ancestors are angry," Anakin boomed, struggling to maintain his act while remaining in the air. "You should flee . . . really quickly."

The Anselmi didn't move.

Anakin had to shake a few trees before they scampered away, the effort nearly sending him crashing back into the pit.

Obi-Wan leapt from the pit, brushing himself off as Anakin lowered himself to solid ground.

"Not bad. Although I worry about you developing a god complex," Obi-Wan said.

"I'm not *that* scary," Anakin said, grinning. "Not if you stay on my good side."

Obi-Wan peered into the pit.

"Perhaps landing wasn't the best idea," he said. "Let's get back in the air."

"I thought you'd never ask," Anakin said, racing for the shuttle.

Soon they were soaring over the ocean once more.

TURN TO PAGE 136.

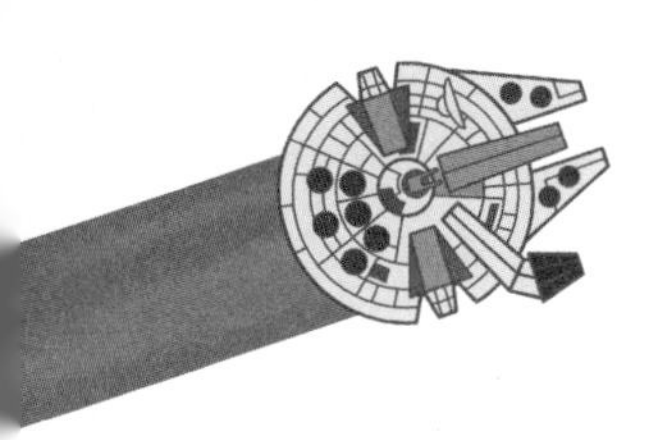

THE GUARD KNOCKED Obi-Wan's lightsaber from his hand. It was now or never. Anakin made his decision and activated the pumps. The water level dropped noticeably within seconds.

The guard glanced up, giving Obi-Wan the opportunity to retaliate. Pushing his opponent back, he plunged into the rapidly diminishing depths to recover his lightsaber. The water was around his shoulders by the time he got back to his feet. Shaking wet hair from his eyes, Obi-Wan brought his lightsaber around. The guard blocked and countered, but Obi-Wan batted the blade away. He attacked again and again, his saber blurring as he forced the guard back.

The kidnapper swept around, but Obi-Wan ducked, the yellow blade passing over his head to carve a molten line along the coral wall. The guard pivoted, bringing both blades to bear, but Obi-Wan was ready. He brought his own lightsaber up, slashing a blade from the guard's gloved hand. Obi-Wan didn't wait for him to retaliate with his other blade, somersaulting over the imposter's head to splash down behind him.

The guard froze as Obi-Wan's lightsaber stopped

centimeters from his neck, the blue glow of the plasma blade reflecting off the Temple Guard mask. All it would take was a flick of Obi-Wan's wrist and the duel would be at an end.

"Drop your weapon," Obi-Wan commanded, and the guard complied, the yellow blade extinguishing as it landed in the water at his feet.

The guard raised gloved hands. "I surrender."

"I'm glad to hear it," Obi-Wan said, still breathing heavily in his helmet. "I've been dying to see who is beneath that mask."

"Then what are you waiting for?" the guard hissed.

Obi-Wan smiled. "I think that honor belongs to my Padawan."

Anakin looked up from the control panel. "Master?"

Obi-Wan arched an eyebrow. "You led us here, Anakin. If you hadn't noticed the markings on the battle droids . . ."

Grinning like a Danorian wolf, Anakin raised a hand and called on the Force. The guard's mask was yanked away, and Anakin's smile dropped.

Obi-Wan's eyes widened as the unmasked guard turned to face him. "No, it can't be. . . ."

"Surprised, Obi?" Bant Eerin said.

"But . . . why?" Obi-Wan stammered, staring at his old friend in disbelief.

The Mon Calamari shook her head. "You still haven't worked it out, have you?"

Obi-Wan's face darkened. Anakin could feel the torment raging in his master, the hurt and anger. Would Obi-Wan strike Bant down where she stood or send her flying into a coral bulkhead in a fit of rage?

Instead, Obi-Wan lowered his lightsaber and delivered his verdict, his voice controlled and steady.

"You will be taken back to Coruscant to stand trial for your crimes."

"I'm afraid that won't happen," a synthesized voice echoed around the base. Anakin and Obi-Wan cried out in shock as their lightsabers were whipped away. The weapons twirled in the air, drawn to a pair of familiar gloved hands.

"Grynask," Anakin hissed as the masked mobster stepped out of the shadows.

"You have Force abilities?" Obi-Wan gasped.

"Of course I do," the Anomid said, reaching up to his mask. There was a click and the crime lord pulled the mask aside to reveal the face of Mace Windu.

"Not you, as well," Obi-Wan groaned, his shoulders slumping. "I don't understand. Why do this? Why kidnap Master Yoda?"

"And why help us back at the temple?" Anakin asked before an idea dawned on him. He thought of the

Jedi Masters watching him in the practice gallery, their eyes narrowed. "Unless," he added, "it was a test . . ."

Obi-Wan frowned at him. "A test?"

"A wise Padawan you have, Obi-Wan," Yoda said from behind the force field.

As they watched, the seaweed bonds fell from the ancient Jedi Master and he hobbled toward them—walking straight through the energy field!

"Master Yoda?" Obi-Wan said.

The old Jedi chuckled. "See your face you should."

"I remember looking at you the same way when *I* faced the test," Mace said.

"As did I," Bant added.

Obi-Wan looked at them. "So all this . . ."

"Was an elaborate ruse, yes," Mace Windu replied, throwing their lightsabers back to them. "And one I have to admit I enjoyed. It's been a long time since I played a new role, although shielding my mind and abilities from you was harder than I thought."

"You should try *fighting* them," Bant pointed out.

Frustration once again flared in Obi-Wan's eyes. "But surely I should have been informed if you were testing my Padawan?"

"Who says the lesson was for him?" Bant said, smiling at her old friend.

Obi-Wan's jaw dropped. "You were testing *me*?"

"For both of you, the test was," Yoda told him.

Mace nodded. "A reminder that while Padawans must listen to their masters . . ."

"Teachers must also listen to their pupils," Bant concluded.

"Much a master can learn from their apprentice," Yoda said, walking toward Obi-Wan. "Work together they must, not argue every step of the way."

"Then I assume we passed?" Obi-Wan said.

Yoda smiled. "A great future you have together. Shape the galaxy, you will."

"I'm glad to hear it."

“It’s just a shame we had to lose our shuttle in the process,” Anakin said.

Obi-Wan raised his eyebrows. “I hope you’re not suggesting we leave it there.”

Anakin groaned. “You want me to lift it back to the surface, don’t you?”

“Yes,” Obi-Wan said, placing a hand on Anakin’s shoulder. “But not on your own.”

Obi-Wan raised his hand toward the sunken ship, looking back at his Padawan. “Ready?”

Smiling, Anakin joined his master and reached out with the Force. “Ready.”

The water outside the base bubbled and churned as the ship rose steadily from the seabed.

That time, neither Anakin nor Obi-Wan cared that they were being watched by the others. All that mattered was that they were working together, not as master and apprentice but as friends . . . brothers.

Anakin hoped it would always be that way.

CONGRATULATIONS, YOU HAVE REACHED THE END OF THE ADVENTURE.

MAY THE FORCE BE WITH YOU.

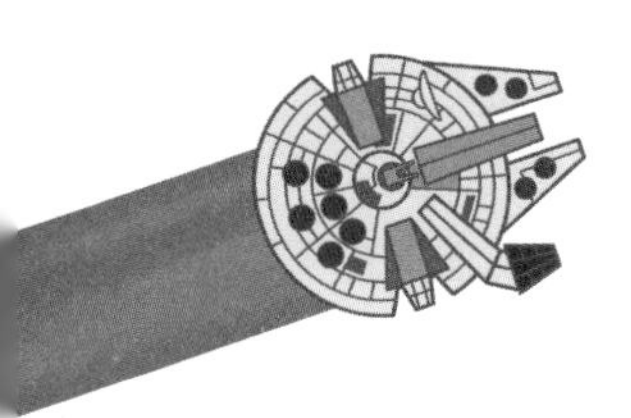

"I'VE HAD ENOUGH of these guys," Anakin said.

"You and me both," Obi-Wan agreed, his lightsaber crackling in the water.

Anakin wasn't one to shy from a fight, but this was a battle even he doubted he could win. Obi-Wan had been right—he wasn't comfortable in the water, and the way the droids moved suggested they'd been reprogrammed for underwater combat.

He looked up to see the whale circling above them.

Maybe it was time for a lesson in beast control.

He reached toward the whale, spreading his fingers wide. He closed his eyes and felt the creature's mind. It was old. Vast. There was something else, an echo of the connection Obi-Wan had established. He sensed how his master had *persuaded* the animal, coaxing it to help. An affinity had formed between them, a bridge between their minds.

Anakin didn't have time for that!

Anakin projected his thoughts through the water, foisting them on the beast.

Your will is my *will. You are mine to command.*

The whale tried to escape, but Anakin wouldn't let go.

No. You must stay here. Attack. Attack!

Nearby, Obi-Wan looked up, shocked. "Anakin, no. That is not the way. A Jedi guides, not controls."

But it was too late. With a howl of anger, the whale came about and charged straight at the battle droids. The robots raised their weapons, the whale's horn spearing the nearest droid while its compatriot fired. The energy harpoon bounced harmlessly off the giant's rocky hide.

"That was unnecessary," Obi-Wan scolded as they swam to the base.

"But it got the job done, didn't it?" Anakin replied. "And no one got hurt . . . except for the droids!"

"Tell that to the whale!" Obi-Wan said, turning his attention to the structure at the bottom of the sea. "But we'll discuss it when we get back to the temple. In the meantime, we need to get into the base."

HOW DO THEY GET IN?

TRY TO USE AN AIRLOCK—TURN TO PAGE 130.

CUT THEIR WAY IN—TURN TO PAGE 112.

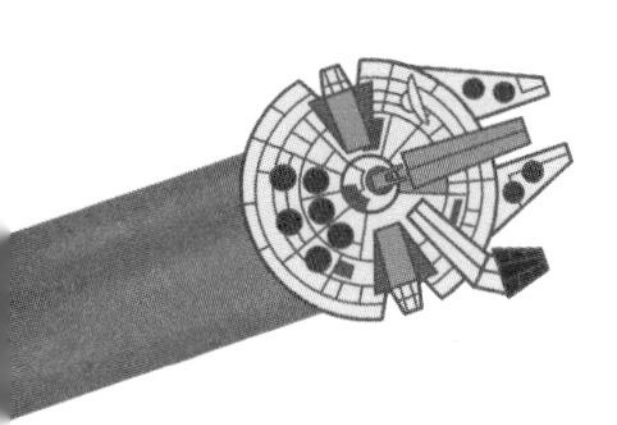

THE FREIGHTER STOOD on a craggy island barely large enough for both vessels.

They landed but found the freighter in lockdown, every hatch sealed tight. Not that that would stop a lightsaber. As Obi-Wan stood guard, Anakin cut a ragged door in the hull.

Using their blades as torches, the Jedi crept through the freighter's low corridors, heading for the flight deck. The craft was abandoned. Frustrated, Anakin slipped behind a computer terminal and tried to bring up the ship's records.

"Blank," he reported. "The databanks have been wiped."

"Just like the droids," Obi-Wan said, noticing a small cloak in a heap on the floor near the pilot's seat. He recovered it, feeling the rough material between his fingers.

"Master Yoda's?" Anakin asked.

Obi-Wan nodded, closing his eyes. Anakin knew he was calling on the Force, attempting to sense the location of the garment's owner.

His eyes snapped open, and he strode from the ship, Anakin scampering after him.

"Obi-Wan? What is it? Do you know where he is?"

For a moment, Anakin thought Obi-Wan was going to step off the side of the island. Instead he stood staring at the water, the cloak still gripped in his hand.

"You think they went down there?"

"This is the only land for miles around."

"Unless they transferred to another ship."

Obi-Wan glanced up at the clear sky. "How many trails did you identify when you scanned for thruster particles?"

"One," Anakin admitted.

"There you have it."

Obi-Wan disappeared into the shuttle, reappearing minutes later with two space helmets complete with breathing apparatuses.

Anakin's heart sank. "You want us to go down there, don't you?"

Obi-Wan arched an eyebrow. "You can swim, can't you?"

Anakin bit his lip. "I can, but . . ."

"But you grew up on a desert planet. I understand, Anakin. Even after all this time, water is strange to you." He looked out over the ocean. "Especially in this quantity. If you're scared . . ."

Anakin snatched the helmet from Obi-Wan's hand. "I'm not scared of anything."

That didn't stop his breath from catching as he lowered the helmet over his head. Obi-Wan checked the seals and told him he would be fine, but Anakin wasn't really listening. He suddenly felt unsteady on his feet.

It wasn't his nerves, though. It was the ground. The entire island was shaking, rising out of the water.

"Perhaps this isn't dry land after all," Obi-Wan said as the guard's freighter was propelled high into the air by a sudden burst of water.

Anakin struggled to keep his balance. "Is that a . . . blowhole?"

"I rather suspect it is," Obi-Wan said before tumbling into the water.

"Obi-Wan!" Anakin yelled, but there was no sign of his master in the roiling water. The rocky ground beneath their feet wasn't rock at all. It was the craggy hide of a gigantic whale!

DO THEY FIGHT THE WHALE?

YES—TURN TO PAGE 108.

NO—TURN TO PAGE 120.

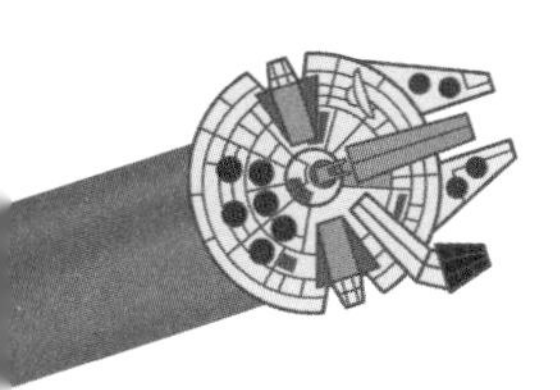

ANAKIN PUSHED OUT with the Force, ripping the seaweed apart. But in his fury, he pushed too hard and the shockwave threw Obi-Wan into nearby rocks.

"Obi-Wan!"

Anakin kicked over to his master. Obi-Wan was unconscious, his fractured helmet filling with water. Anakin looked around, but the guard was nowhere to be seen. It didn't matter. He had to save Obi-Wan.

Grabbing hold of the Jedi's robe, Anakin hauled Obi-Wan back up to the surface, his arms and legs burning from the effort.

Anakin felt rather than heard the explosion far below. Seconds later, a spaceship burst from the ocean to shoot into the sky, the same spaceship Anakin had chased on Coruscant.

The blast must have been the guard covering his tracks. They were back to square one, with no more leads to follow.

THE END

CAN YOU HELP ANAKIN MAKE BETTER CHOICES?

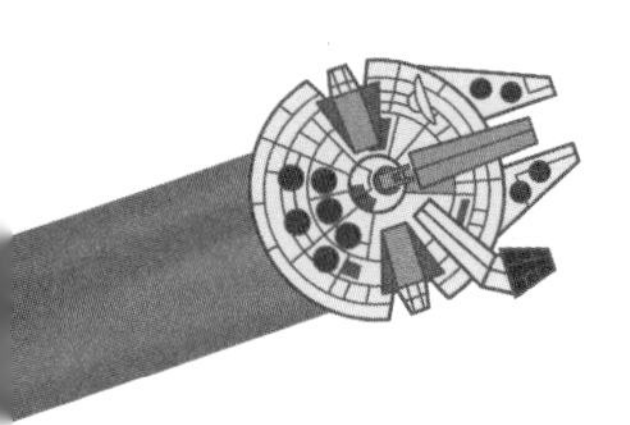

ANAKIN PLUNGED INTO THE WATER, lightsaber already in hand. The whale crashed beneath the surface, sending him tumbling head over heels. He flailed in the churning water, looking desperately for Obi-Wan. All he could see was the monstrous creature that had dumped them into the sea. It was huge, with long tentacles and rows of eyes along its slablike head. It opened its mouth, revealing teeth the size of rancors.

Anakin propelled himself forward, holding his lightsaber out like a spear. He had no idea if the blade would slice through the whale's calcified hide, but he had to try.

He never got a chance. The whale moved faster than Anakin had thought possible, swinging around to face him. Its terrifying maw yawned open, and Anakin was washed inside.

He was being swallowed whole!

He fought against the tide, but there was nothing he could do. He splashed into a vast, stinking chamber, but it was no cave. He was quite literally in the belly of the beast.

"Well, that went well."

It was Obi-Wan, standing knee-high in briny water, his lightsaber gleaming in the darkness.

"How are we going to get out?" Anakin asked, his own lightsaber lost somewhere down the monster's gullet.

"With extreme difficulty," Obi-Wan replied gravely.

THE END

CAN YOU HELP ANAKIN MAKE BETTER CHOICES?

"LEAVE THIS TO ME."

Anakin kicked off of the wall to attack the guard. As if sensing him coming, the guard flicked around, a boot meeting Anakin's helmet. The blow sent Anakin into a spin, his lightsaber flying from his hand. He reached after it, calling the weapon back to him, but his eyes went wide as one of the guard's yellow blades sliced Anakin's lightsaber in two.

Shaking with fury, Anakin propelled himself forward to grapple with the traitor. They tumbled in the water, Anakin catching a glimpse of Obi-Wan.

The Jedi Knight had tried to lower the energy field and, frustrated with his lack of progress, was about to plunge his lightsaber into the mechanism.

He didn't know about the thermal detonator.

"Obi-Wan, don't—" Anakin yelled, but his warning was lost in the explosion.

Anakin groaned, turning over on the wet deck of the Jedi shuttle. Obi-Wan lay beside him, robes tattered and face blackened.

They looked at each other in confusion. Who was flying the ship?

"Disappointed I am," came a familiar voice from the pilot's seat. Yoda operated the controls with the Force, yanking back the hyperdrive lever.

"M-Master Yoda?" Obi-Wan stammered, grabbing the back of a chair to haul himself up. "How . . . ?"

"How did we escape, hmm?" the Grand Master said. "Forced to rescue my rescuers, I was. Why? Because still you do not work as a team. Still you do not listen. Learned nothing you have. Learn nothing you will."

An uncomfortable silence fell over the flight deck, and Yoda's condemnation echoed in their ears.

THE END

CAN YOU HELP ANAKIN AND OBI-WAN MAKE BETTER CHOICES?

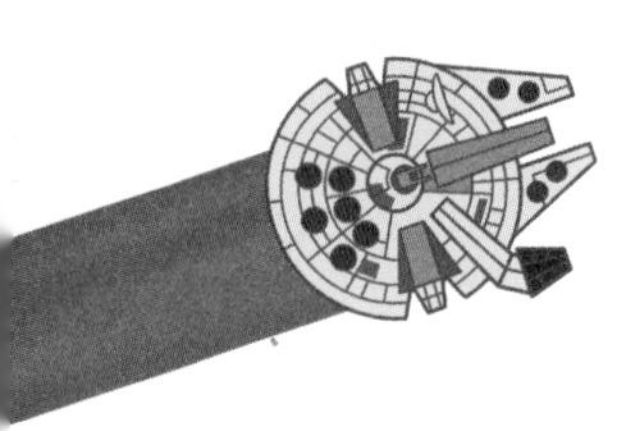

BEFORE OBI-WAN COULD STOP HIM, Anakin plunged his lightsaber into the side of the coral dome, tracing a jagged line through the curved wall.

Water gushed into the base, taking them with it.

Obi-Wan grabbed a panel on the wall, trying to stand as the water levels rose to their waists. "I was hoping we could get in *without* flooding everything."

"Where's the fun in that?" Anakin asked, splashing down a corridor, the water up to his chest.

Before long they were back to swimming, propelling themselves around the drowned base—but this time, Anakin knew exactly where he was heading. He could feel a familiar presence up ahead.

"Master Yoda!"

They found the Jedi floating behind a crackling energy field, his arms bound by thick seaweed and his eyes closed.

The Jedi Master was suspended in a large air bubble.

"Why didn't I think of that?" Anakin said, impressed as always with the Grand Master's mastery of the Force.

"Holding back an ocean is no easy task," scolded

Obi-Wan. He reached out, testing the stretch of the energy field. It fizzed beneath his hand. "Perhaps you could put *your* talents to use and lower this energy field?"

Anakin swam over to the wall and found a control panel set into the coral. He reached for his bit driver, but the tool was no longer in his pouch. It must have been washed away when they submerged.

HOW SHOULD ANAKIN SHUT DOWN THE ENERGY FIELD?

BURN OUT THE MECHANISM WITH HIS LIGHTSABER—TURN TO PAGE 125.

TRY TO REWIRE IT—GO TO PAGE 126.

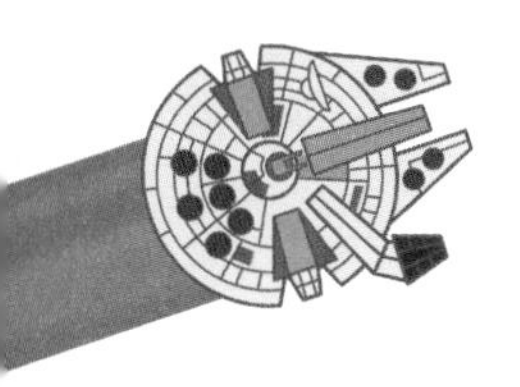

ANAKIN TRIED TO BLOCK an energy harpoon. On dry land, he would have deflected the shot easily, but fighting underwater was another matter. The bolt slammed into his shoulder, spinning him around.

Another shot struck him in the back, propelling him into the rough coral wall, which cracked his helmet.

He felt a tremor in the Force as Obi-Wan shoved the droids back. Then Obi-Wan dragged Anakin back up to the surface and tugged his broken helmet free. Anakin coughed up seawater as he felt Obi-Wan sending out a telepathic cry for help.

Anakin's wounded and we've lost our ship. Please, come quickly.

But Anakin felt another presence—Mace Windu, closer than they could have hoped.

I'm coming for you. It shouldn't have gone this far. . . .

Anakin didn't know what Mace meant. He just knew they'd be safe soon. That was all that mattered.

THE END

CAN YOU HELP ANAKIN MAKE BETTER CHOICES?

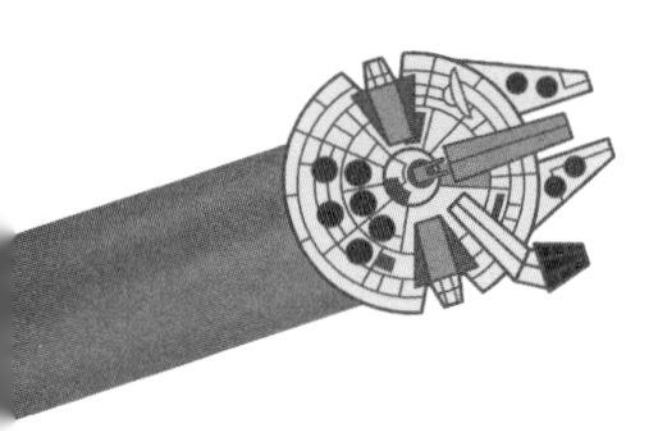

DON'T GET DISTRACTED, Anakin told himself. He pushed on, trying to trick the computer into lowering the energy field. The shield crackled and dissipated. Anakin freed Yoda with a swipe of his lightsaber. The seaweed bonds fell away, and Yoda opened his eyes, maintaining the air pocket.

"About time, it is."

Grinning, Anakin turned back to the fight, finding only Obi-Wan clutching his own arm. There was no sign of the traitorous guard.

"You let him get away," Anakin snapped.

"I didn't have much choice," Obi-Wan said, his fingers covering a deep cut in his arm.

"So we *still* don't know who it was. Did you at least see which way he went?"

Obi-Wan kicked himself into the air pocket. "I was too busy trying not to get killed."

"You should have called for help."

"And what exactly could you have done?"

"What's that supposed to mean?"

"You let him escape once before. What makes you think you could stop him this time?"

“Silence!”

Master Yoda’s shout had the desired effect. Neither Jedi had ever heard the Grand Master raise his voice like that. “Tolerate this constant bickering I will not,” he told them, and he hobbled away, taking his air pocket with him. “Return to Coruscant we must.”

Anakin watched him go before turning to his master. “Is that it? We’re not even going to get a thank-you?”

“Oh, be quiet, Anakin,” Obi-Wan said, swimming after Yoda.

THE END

CAN YOU HELP ANAKIN MAKE BETTER CHOICES?

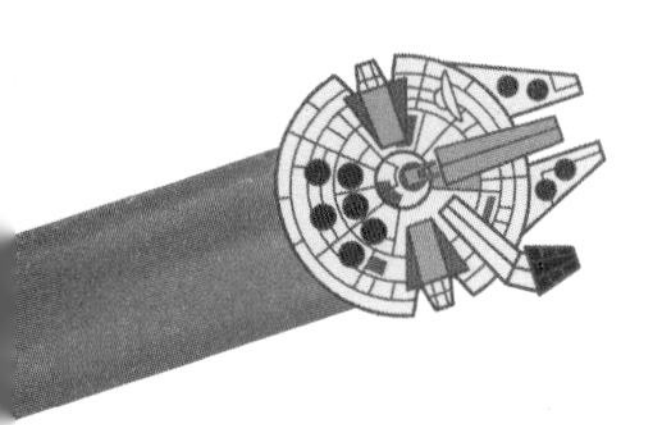

"IT'S BEAUTIFUL," Anakin exclaimed as the shuttle dipped into Glee Anselm's atmosphere.

Obi-Wan agreed. "A veritable paradise."

Crystal blue seas stretched below them, dotted by tiny tropical islands. The planet had no major landmasses, which meant no one ever really went there. The denizens of Glee Anselm had little interest in trading with the galaxy at large, and the planet had yet to become a tourist trap. Its handful of beaches, shimmering with golden sand, were untouched, and crested reptavians soared through the sapphire skies.

"This is Kit Fisto's home, right?" Anakin asked as the shuttle skimmed the water.

Obi-Wan nodded. "Yes. The Nautolans are the primary species, dwelling largely beneath the waves, although some Anselmi still survive."

"Anselmi?"

"Land dwellers, unable to breathe underwater."

Anakin gazed over the boundless oceans. "Not much land to go around."

Obi-Wan nodded. "It does put them at something of a disadvantage, yes. Legend has it that there used to be a vast continent teeming with life, but it sank to the seabed millennia ago."

"It's certainly a big planet," Anakin said. "Where do we start?"

WHERE SHOULD THEY SEARCH FIRST?

THE OCEAN—TURN TO PAGE 136.

THE LAND—GO TO PAGE 131.

ANAKIN WATCHED in horror as their shuttle slid from the whale's back and tumbled into the water.

He followed seconds later, diving for cover as the sea giant crashed beneath the waves with a deafening roar.

The water churned in the whale's wake, and the monster's gargantuan body filled Anakin's vision, spiraled tusks to seething mass of tentacles that thrashed where a tail would have been.

Anakin ducked, narrowly avoiding being whacked in the face by a sucker the size of a radar dish.

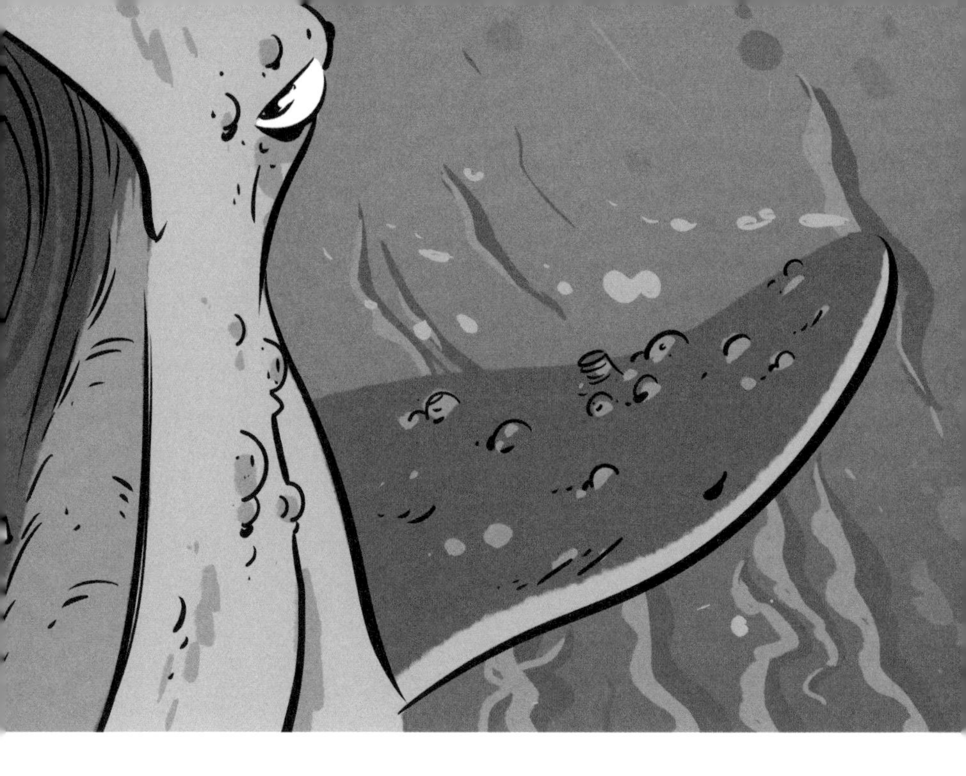

Something closed around his wrist. He tried to pull free but was jerked around to face Obi-Wan.

"Try not to panic," the Jedi said over their helmets' comlink.

"Try not to panic?" Anakin snapped, yanking his arm from Obi-Wan's grip. "Have you seen the size of that thing's *teeth*?"

"Yes. I'm looking at them right now."

Anakin swam around to see the whale rushing toward them, its mouth open wide.

Anakin went for his lightsaber.

"No!" Obi-Wan said. "We don't want to antagonize it."

"We landed a ship on its back!" Anakin spluttered, trying to pull Obi-Wan away. "We need to move."

"No," Obi-Wan said, swatting Anakin's hands away. "We're exactly where we're supposed to be."

"It's going to ram us!"

"I sincerely hope so," Obi-Wan said, opening his arms as if to welcome an old friend.

It was like being hit by a sandcrawler. Anakin was sure he heard his helmet crack as the whale careened into them. They were pushed along, flattened against the whale's head like dust flies on a landspeeder's viewscreen.

And that was what Obi-Wan wanted?

Sometimes Anakin wondered if he'd ever understand his master.

"That's it," Obi-Wan said over the comm. "Good boy."

Good boy?

The whale slowed. Anakin forced his head around to witness Obi-Wan stroking the beast's rocklike skin as if it was a voorpak. "What are you doing?"

"Making a new friend. You better hang on."

"To what?"

Obi-Wan gripped one of the whale's thick tusks,

indicating that Anakin should do the same. No sooner were Anakin's fingers wrapped around the ivory tusk than the beast plunged into a stomach-lurching dive.

"Where is it taking us?"

"To meet its master!" Obi-Wan yelled back, nodding toward a large shell on the seabed. It was the size of a hangar, lights blinking on its luminescent walls. Anakin peered closer, noticing pipes anchoring it to the seabed.

That wasn't a shell. It was an underwater base, constructed . . . no, *grown* from glowing coral.

The whale slowed, a deep groan reverberating through its body.

"Time to get off," Obi-Wan said, pushing free of the beast.

Anakin did likewise, spotting their shuttle lying upside down nearby. As he watched, a striped eel emerged from the ship's open hatch, followed by a shoal of silver fish.

"Oh, great," he groaned "The hyperdrive's bound to be flooded . . . along with everything else!"

"I suggest we worry about that later," Obi-Wan said, reaching for his lightsaber. "If there *is* a later!"

Anakin turned to see a pair of aquatic battle droids streaking toward them, propelled by bubbling jet packs and hefting energy harpoons that looked ready to tear them apart.

DO THEY FIGHT THE DROIDS OR TRY TO GET INTO THE BASE?

FIGHT THE DROIDS—TURN TO PAGE 115.

GET INTO THE BASE—GO TO PAGE 102.

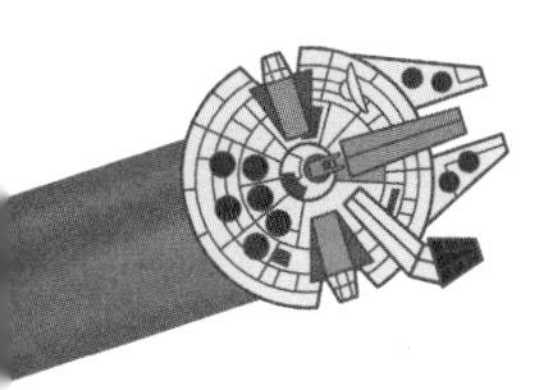

THEY WERE RUNNING OUT OF TIME. Anakin plunged his lightsaber into the lock.

If he had waited just a second, he would have felt a warning from the Force. He would have sensed the thermal detonator hidden among the wires.

He would have avoided setting off the explosion that ripped the base apart.

TURN TO PAGE 132.

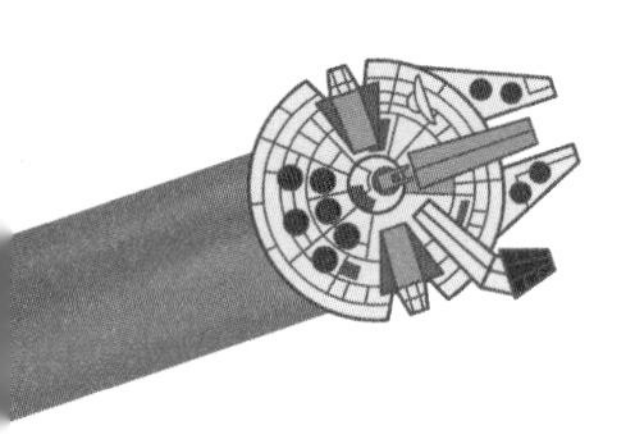

HE WAS ABOUT TO REACH for his lightsaber when he sensed something was wrong. Prying open the access port, he pulled a clump of wires aside to reveal a thermal detonator wedged at the back of the control panel. The mechanism had been booby-trapped! It was lucky he hadn't plunged his lightsaber into the lock.

"Well?" Obi-Wan asked.

"It's going to take slightly longer than I thought," Anakin admitted, trying to cram his fingers into the access port.

"Time you do not have, Jedi brat," a modulated voice hissed over their comms.

They turned to find Yoda's kidnapper floating behind them, two halves of a scorched lightsaber pike held tight in his gauntleted hands.

With a sizzling thrum, the Temple Guard activated the yellow plasma blades.

WHAT SHOULD ANAKIN DO?

FIGHT THE GUARD—GO TO PAGE 110.

CONCENTRATE ON DISARMING THE ENERGY FIELD—TURN TO PAGE 127.

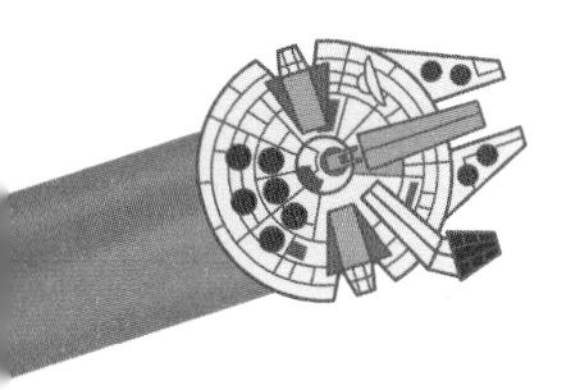

OBI-WAN LAUNCHED himself at the guard.

Anakin's mentor was a seasoned member of the Order and well trained in the Jedi arts, but the rogue Temple Guard seemed to be just as skilled.

The young Jedi watched as the guard parried every one of Obi-Wan's blows, moving in the water with more grace than Anakin had expected . . . or could hope to replicate himself.

Anakin's first instinct was to jump in and assist with the attack, but Obi-Wan and the guard were well matched. Obi-Wan could handle himself, plus Anakin had a job to do.

He turned back to the controls, trying to ignore the sounds of the fight that filtered through his comlink. He flicked on a screen and realized that the force field was protected by reams of binary code.

This was going to take forever!

Undaunted, he probed deeper, hoping that his meddling wouldn't activate the booby trap.

Behind him, Obi-Wan was beginning to tire. His breathing had become ragged and his movements sluggish.

Obi-Wan's opponent, on the other hand, looked completely at home, twirling in the water like an Anjolan dancer. He was slowly wearing Obi-Wan down, strike by strike. But the Jedi Knight called on the Force to guide him, moving with the current to block the guard's yellow blades and attack.

Text scrolled down the screen, and Anakin's eyes went wide.

Forget the force field . . . he could access the base's main systems from there, including the environmental systems!

That meant he could drain the base, pumping the water back out into the ocean.

The guard's advantage over Obi-Wan would be lost—but what about the force field?

WHAT SHOULD ANAKIN DO?

FREE YODA BY LOWERING THE FORCE FIELD—GO TO PAGE 116.

HELP OBI-WAN BY PUMPING OUT THE WATER—GO TO PAGE 96.

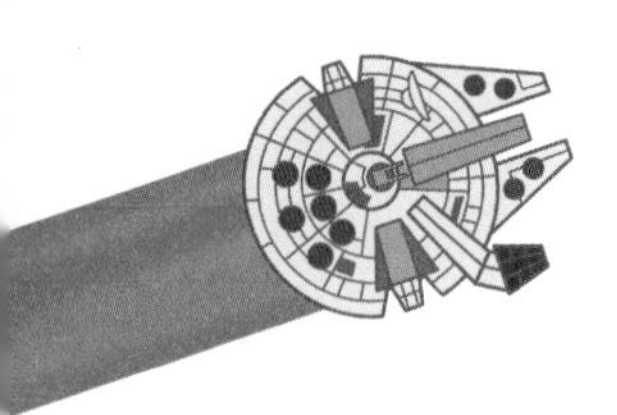

"OVER HERE!"

Obi-Wan had found an airlock, the thick glass crusted with barnacles.

"How do you open it?" Anakin asked, checking the circular door.

"There," Obi-Wan said, brushing away some shells to reveal a keypad on the other side of the reinforced glass.

The Jedi closed his eyes. In the base, the keys beeped as if pressed by invisible fingers.

"You're going to *guess* the combination?"

"The Force will guide me," Obi-Wan replied, trying another sequence.

A bellow echoed through the water. Anakin could feel the whale panicking. The aquatic droid was getting the upper hand.

Obi-Wan continued to manipulate the keys. "Almost there."

WHAT DOES ANAKIN DO?

WAIT FOR OBI-WAN TO GUESS THE CODE—GO TO PAGE 134.

CUT HIS WAY INTO THE BASE—TURN TO PAGE 112.

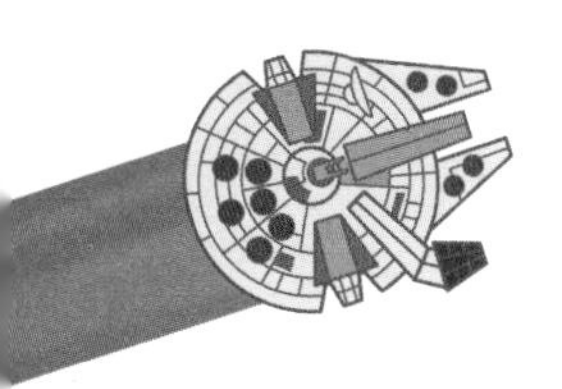

"BRING US DOWN THERE," Obi-Wan said, pointing to an island covered in dense forest.

But as they stepped off the shuttle, they tumbled into a deep pit that had been hidden under palm leaves.

Obi-Wan and Anakin looked up to see squat figures peering into the pit. They looked not unlike Nautolans, although they lacked the long head tentacles of their aquatic cousins.

"The Anselmi?" Anakin guessed.

Obi-Wan nodded, looking along the row of sharp arrows pointing down at them. "According to Kit Fisto, they're a superstitious lot, little more than savages."

"Welcome, honored sacrifices," cried an Anselmi.

"Sacrifices?" Obi-Wan said.

"You shall be offered to the spirits of our ancestors. Only then will we be victorious over the gill heads."

WHAT DOES ANAKIN DO?

LEAP OUT OF THE PIT AND FIGHT—TURN TO PAGE 138.

TRY TO TRICK THE ANSELMI—GO TO PAGE 94.

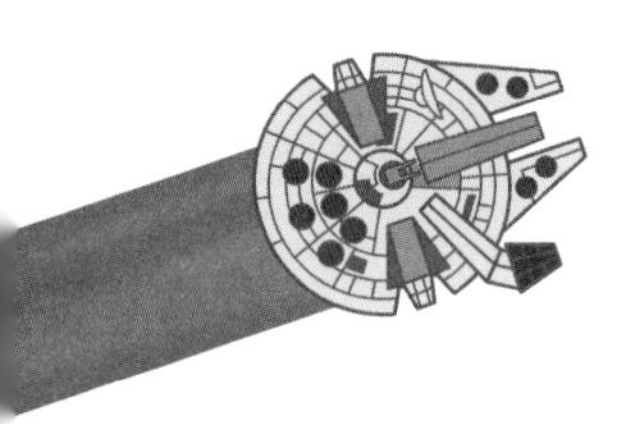

ANAKIN AWOKE WITH THE SUN beating down on him and sand scraping his cheek.

He sat up, his head spinning with the sudden movement.

"Steady," Obi-Wan said. "You're lucky to be alive."

Anakin looked around at the empty beach. "I . . . I don't remember what happened."

"I swam us to safety."

"And the guard?"

Obi-Wan sighed. "Gone . . . without a trace."

Anakin lay back on the sand and looked up at the lizard-gulls wheeling high above. "And Master Yoda, too."

"And this time," Obi-Wan said, the disappointment clear in his voice, "we have no leads to follow. . . ."

THE END

CAN YOU HELP ANAKIN AND OBI-WAN MAKE BETTER CHOICES?

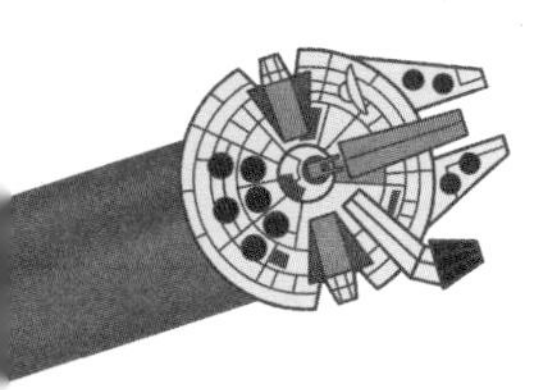

“OBI-WAN!”

The Jedi Knight kicked his legs, propelling himself back toward Anakin. His lightsaber flashed, and the seaweed drifted apart, sliced cleanly in two.

“Where’s the guard?”

They looked up to see the traitor escaping on the back of the whale, beside a familiar figure wrapped in seaweed.

“Master Yoda!” Anakin called out, swimming after the beast.

Behind him, Obi-Wan paused, looking at the base in concern. Anakin felt it, too, a sudden warning on the edge of his consciousness.

The base erupted in a fireball that was immediately extinguished by the depths. That didn’t stop Anakin and Obi-Wan from being knocked back by the shockwave. Anakin hit a jagged rock, and everything went dark.

TURN TO PAGE 132.

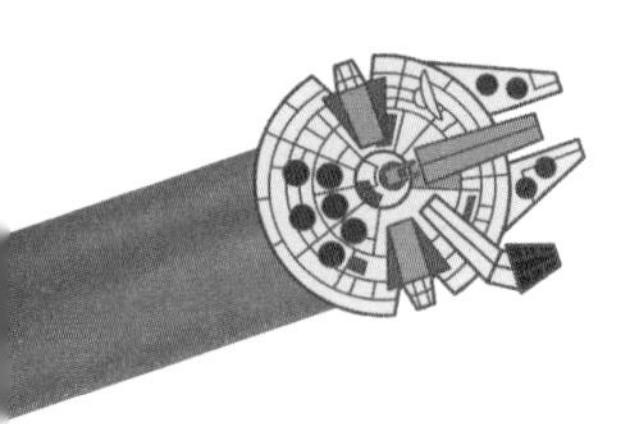

A SIREN BLARED inside the base.

"You've triggered an alarm!" Anakin shouted.

Obi-Wan opened his eyes. "Everyone's a critic."

The airlock slid open and the traitorous Temple Guard shot toward them like a torpedo, a yellow blade glowing in each hand. It was a sight to behold, but Anakin and Obi-Wan would not go down without a fight.

"Two against one," Anakin said, drawing his own lightsaber.

"It hardly seems fair," Obi-Wan agreed, adopting a defensive stance.

The guard corkscrewed, energy blades crackling in the water.

The Jedi tried to defend themselves, but the guard moved with grace and dexterity, easily avoiding their clumsy attacks.

Obi-Wan cried out as the guard flipped over and caught the Jedi's chest with a boot.

His helmet fogging, Anakin lunged forward, but he was too slow.

The guard brought up an arm, revealing a catapult

attached to one wrist. It fired a seedlike projectile that struck Anakin in the chest.

Tendrils of writhing seaweed burst from the pellet, trapping Anakin in a living net.

WHAT DOES ANAKIN DO?

CALL FOR HELP—TURN TO PAGE 133.

BREAK OUT USING THE FORCE—GO TO PAGE 107.

THE SHUTTLE SOARED across the water, the rolling sea stretching to the horizon.

"There's nothing but water," Anakin sighed. "How are we going to find the kidnapper?"

"Maybe we're searching for the wrong person," Obi-Wan replied. "If Yoda *was* brought here . . ."

Anakin perked up. "We might be able to sense *him*!"

Obi-Wan nodded, proud of his Padawan.

"Indeed. Now, concentrate."

Anakin relaxed, closing his eyes. He felt the planet all around him. Lizard-gulls in the air, giant eels in the sea. He felt the coolness of the ocean spray against his face and the warmth of the bright sun against his neck.

And all the time he imagined Master Yoda's impossibly old face. Those wise eyes. That impish smile. The sound of a twisted cane *tap-tap-tap*ping on the temple flagstones.

There was nothing.

"He's not here," Anakin sighed.

Beside him, Obi-Wan was still meditating. "Don't give up so soon. You can do this, Anakin."

“I know I can,” Anakin snapped, flicking switches to activate the ship’s sensor array.

“I’ve got him!” he suddenly announced.

“What did I tell you?” Obi-Wan opened his eyes. “If we trust in the Force . . .”

His face fell as he saw Anakin peering at a nearby display. “Oh. You used the shuttle.”

“I remembered what you said about no one coming here and searched for thruster particles in the atmosphere. . . .”

“Especially a thruster damaged while fleeing the scene of a crime,” Obi-Wan muttered, his arms crossed over his chest.

“Transferring data to the navicomputer,” Anakin said, operating the shuttle’s systems with finesse.

They didn’t have to fly for long. “There it is,” Anakin said, pointing out a small island on the horizon. “The ship from the temple! See?”

TURN TO PAGE 104.

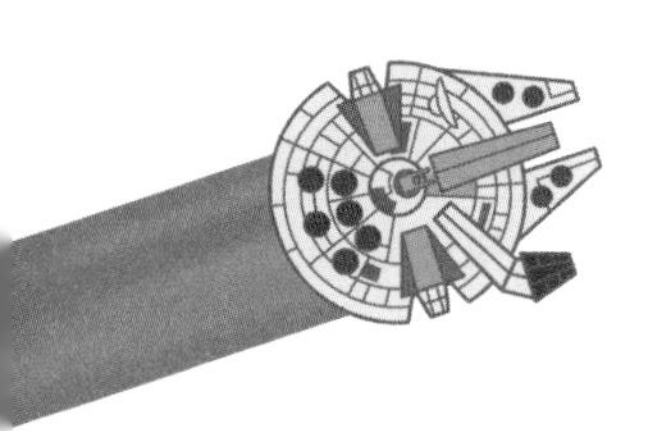

"LIKE I'M GOING TO BE threatened by you!" Anakin shouted, leaping out of the pit.

The Anselmi fired, but Anakin's lightsaber made short work of the arrows.

He landed in their midst, pushing out with the Force before they could regroup. Half the hunters tumbled into the pit, where Obi-Wan was waiting—but there were no sounds of battle. What was Obi-Wan doing down there?

Something sharp jabbed into his neck. Anakin swatted at the sudden pain, thinking it was a bug, but found a sharp thorn embedded in his skin. He looked up to see the Anselmi leader lowering a blowpipe from her lips.

Anakin's lightsaber slipped from his fingers, and he tumbled forward, completely paralyzed.

So that was what had happened to Obi-Wan.

Maybe, just this once, attack hadn't been the best form of defense.

THE END

CAN YOU HELP ANAKIN MAKE BETTER CHOICES?

CAVAN SCOTT is one of the writers of *Star Wars*: Adventures in Wild Space and IDW Publishing's *Star Wars* Adventures comic book series. When he's not playing in a galaxy far, far away, Cavan has also written for such popular franchises as Doctor Who, Pacific Rim, The Incredibles, Ghostbusters, Adventure Time, and Penguins of Madagascar. You can find him online at www.cavanscott.com.

ELSA CHARRETIER is a French comic book artist and comic book writer. After debuting on C.O.W.L. at Image Comics, Elsa cocreated The Infinite Loop with writer Pierrick Colinet at IDW. She has worked at DC Comics (Starfire, Bombshells, Harley Quinn), launched The Unstoppable Wasp at Marvel, and recently completed the art for the adaptation of *Windhaven* by George R. R. Martin and Lisa Tuttle (Bantam Books). She is currently writing two creator-owned series and has illustrated the first issue of *Star Wars*: Forces of Destiny for IDW.